THE GOSPEL YOU ARE BEING TAUGHT,

THE TRUE GOSPEL OF JESUS CHRIST?

the beginning is wrong, does that change the ending?

FROM THE AUTHOR: THIS BOOK IS DOCTRINALLY HERETICAL.
READ AT YOUR OWN RISK

AARON STANDBERRY

WORKBOOK PRESS LLC
187 E Warm Springs Rd,
Suite B285, Las Vegas, NV 89119, USA

Website: https://workbookpress.com/
Hotline: 1-888-818-4856
Email: admin@workbookpress.com

Ordering Information:
Quantity sales. Special discounts are available on quantity purchases by corporations, associations, and others.
For details, contact the publisher at the address above.

Library of Congress Control Number:

ISBN-13:   000-0-000000-00-0 (Paperback Version)
                000-0-000000-00-0 (Digital Version)

REV. DATE: 05/25/2022

IS THE GOSPEL YOU ARE BEING TAUGHT THE TRUE GOSPEL OF JESUS CHRIST?

If the beginning is wrong, does that change the ending?

Aaron Standberry

"John L. Standberry Sr. taught me to be the best at whatever I did."

"John L. Standberry Jr. taught me that dreams can be reached."

John Lester Standberry III coined the message, "FREE YOUR MIND"

JESUS THE CHRIST TAUGHT ME THAT "I CAN DO ALL THINGS IN HIM".

FOREWORD

Trevor Smith

5.0 out of 5 stars **An Unconventional Yet Thought Provoking Interpretation**

Reviewed in the United States on April 1, 2021

Standberry, a long-time pastor and student of scripture, has created a work that challenges many conventionally held views regarding Christ and his connection to Old Testament philosophy. Asserting that the early books of the Bible tend to be selectively interpreted to create a popular, rather than accurate, narrative, Standberry challenges the reader to re-examine scripture in a more wholistic manner. His interpretations, although somewhat unconventional, are nonetheless grounded in the direct language of the Bible, and are quite though provoking. Of note he asserts that much of what is written is merely overlooked because it is considered unimportant, or perhaps is uncomfortable for modern Christians to embrace. This work is a good read for any biblical scholar, or person of faith that seeks to expand his/her views on scripture. It may change minds, or merely serve as an interesting though experiment. In either case, it draws one to better respect the fact that Biblical writings are far more complex than many assume, and still have many lessons to reveal.

Brian Carriere

5.0 out of 5 stars **Be Prepared to Doubt Your Beliefs**

Reviewed in the United States on May 2, 2021

Standberry offers a new perspective and challenges readers to think critically about what they have been taught regarding the Holy Bible. Standberry is a pastor and perpetual student of scripture, as well as US veteran. Christians today are often more concerned with perception than reality. Many focus more on man, preacher, or politician. They appear Christian-like but in their hearts Christ knows they are yet pure. Standberry challenges each of us to consider whether we are true Christians or simply pretending to be so. This approach is likely to make many feel uncomfortable but those who seek true faith will be well served to read this work, perhaps multiple times, and contemplate the questions being posed.

FOREWORD TAKEN FROM AMAZON BOOK REVIEWS

CONTENTS

WARNING

A word of caution to whoever may be reading this. The information in this narrative is Bible-based, although some of it is based on the science of today. It has been integrated into the narrative as a point of comparison between secular and religious teachings and methods. All writings here are from the inspiration given to me by the Lord Jesus, the Christ. Please check all the posted Scriptures before you make an opinion or try to label it or me. My Scripture guidance comes from Galatians 1:6–12 (KJV):

> I marvel that ye are so soon removed from him that called you into the grace of Christ unto another gospel: Which is not another; but there be some that trouble you, and would pervert the gospel of Christ. But though we, or an angel from heaven, preach any other gospel unto you than that which we have preached unto you, let him be accursed. As we said before, so say I now again, if any man preach any other gospel unto you than that ye have received, let him be accursed. For do I now persuade men, or God? or do I seek to please men? for if I yet pleased men, I should not be the servant of Christ. *But I certify you, brethren, that the gospel which was preached of me is not after man. For I neither received it of man, neither was I taught it, but by the revelation of Jesus Christ.* (Emphasis mine)

Thank you,
Aaron Standberry

IS THE DOCTRINE YOU ARE TAUGHT THE TRUE GOSPEL OF CHRIST?

The Free Will of Man

Today, those of us who declare ourselves as being Christian (believers) get all kinds of doctrinal teachings preached to us. We get a word about how to be prosperous, how to get great power, how the church is failing, etc. Many of our doctrinal preachers have become motivational speakers (encouraging us to tell our neighbor this or that, when to say amen, or speak this way or that). The most taught doctrine is the belief in "man's free will." Because this is common teaching, I did some research and this is what I discovered: Oftentimes, when I discuss with believers the different aspects of Scriptures, the conversation normally leads to the "free will of man" doctrine. I have found that many times people use this phrase to explain a doctrine of man's partnership with God: the belief that God will not force us to do anything against our will (because we are not robots). This conclusion is the mainstream understanding of how man relates to God.

The Contrast of Creatures

If we explore 2 Corinthians 5, we find Paul appealing to the nature of those who are in Christ. He indicates that it is better to be out of the body because to be so is to be in the presence of the Lord. Paul tells us that whatever state we are in, our objective is to be accepted by the Lord. As he continues, it is noted that all of us will stand before the Lord to receive those things done in the body either good or bad. However, his primary point is that those who are in Christ have died to the things of the world and have become new creatures. Please understand that he did not say a new man but a new creature. A creation that has a whole different category. A category that is of God, where all things have become new. Using this wisdom, a person who is a new creature only serves the will of God. You may ask, what is the will of God for us? In 2 Corinthians 5:18, it tell us that we have been given a ministry of reconciliation. This ministry is the same as Jesus's ministry, which was to reconcile the world unto himself.

Precepts of Reconciliation

Now, there are two precepts to this reconciliation: one is that we (believers) are constrained (held together) by the love of Christ and the other is that we are not to impute their (the unlearned or unbelievers; 1 Cor. 14:23) transgressions unto them. In the second precept, we are told not to tabulate, reckon, compute, calculate, or to tabulate over anyone trespasses (*Strong's Concordance*, G3049). My understanding of this passage is not to bring up their past transgressions. In John 3:18, we are told that those who believe are not condemned, but those that believe not (unbelievers) are already condemned. Now the question is, can an unbeliever get saved? If so, who is able to save them? First of all, let us look at John 3:18 and the word *condemned*. *Strong's Concordance* G2919 explains the word *condemned* is to be separate, put asunder, to pick out, select, or to choose. It goes on to indicate that this is an act of pronouncing judgment. The *Concordance* indicates that this is a root word, and the meaning is final. Also, another word to focus on is *unbeliever*. *Strong's Concordance* states that an "unbeliever" (G571) is someone who is unfaithful, faithless, and not to be trusted; they are incredulous and without trust in God. On the other hand, an unlearned person, *Strong's Concordance* G62 means to be illiterate. The dictionary defines "illiterate" as "having or demonstrating very little or no education, showing a lack of culture, especially in language and literature, and displaying a marked lack of knowledge in a particular field." If we look at Genesis 4:19, 23–24, Lamech, Cain's (who was condemned by God) descendant, declared what he had done was more terrible than his Cain's; he then pronounced that he accepted the sentence of Cain, which was to be separated from God and given a covering mark. This made him feel better than all others. Therefore, a condemned person is an unbeliever of this mind-set and must not be trusted. The reason this matter is that many have confused an unlearned person from an unbeliever. An unlearned can become a believer but an unbeliever cannot. This is because an unbeliever has a reprobate mind; given to him by God in Romans 1:28. Also, in 2 Thessalonians 2:11, God sends them a strong delusion to believe a lie. That lie was the mindset of Lamech. Now, the answer to the question is that an unbeliever cannot be converted; because they have been turned over to a strong delusion by God. The final answer to this question comes from John 12:38–41, where he quotes Isaiah 6:10 in New Testament understanding, "That the saying of Esaias the prophet might be fulfilled, which he spake, Lord, who hath believed our report? and to whom hath the arm of the Lord been revealed? Therefore, they could not believe, because that Esaias said again. He hath blinded their eyes, and hardened their heart; that they should not see with their eyes, nor understand with their heart, and be converted, and I should heal them. These things said Esaias, when he saw his glory, and spake of him." This revelation bring up an ideal question. The question is, Was the turning over to a reprobate mind in Romans 1 by God, the action taken in Genesis 6 when God removed his Spirit from all but Noah? Now my point is this: if we (believers) are to be ambassadors for Christ, then the only will we have is his will, which is to reconcile those who are his, to their remembrance of who they are, and whom they are (Luke 15:17–20).

The Judgment

From 2 Corinthians 5:10, we also understand that there is a judgment that goes along with all of this. The judgment will be standing before the judgment seat of Christ in order to receive rewards. Rewards for what has been done in the body, both good and bad. If we look at Matthew 25:45–46, the King issues out judgment on to those on his right hand and those on his left hand. His final judgment is identified in verses 45–46. Therefore, the rewards mentioned in 2 Corinthians 5 are everlasting punishment to those on the left hand and everlasting life to those on the right. You do remember what Matthew 25:31–33 identifies, "When the Son of man shall come in his glory, and all the holy angels with him, then shall he sit upon the throne of his glory: And before him shall be gathered all nations: and he shall separate them one from another, as a shepherd divideth his sheep from the goats: And he shall set the sheep on his right hand, but the goats on the left." This runs parallel to what the King did. Anyhow, we must note that the King did not say those who did it sometimes. Jesus confirmed this in Matthew 13:47–50 when he told the disciples what the kingdom of heaven was like. He said, "Again, the kingdom of heaven is like unto, a net, that was cast into the sea and gathered of every kind: Which when it was full, they drew to shore, and sat down, and gathered the good into vessels, but cast the bad away. So shall it be at the end of the world: the angels shall come forth, and sever the wicked from among the just, And shall cast them into the furnace of fire: there shall be wailing and gnashing of teeth." Therefore, in order to be who Jesus says we are, we must do only his will, which is the will of righteousness. Paul tells us in Romans 8:19 that the earnest expectation of the creatures is that the sons of God manifest themselves. We know this action will liberate the creatures from their bondage of selfishness. We know that God has already put all things in subjection under his (man) feet (Heb. 2:8). The question is when did that happen? Was it in the beginning, at the cross, or is it yet to come? Looking at verse 7, it mentions that God gave the works of his hand to the man. Therefore, everything mentioned is about in the beginning, when man Adam became a *living soul.* More on this later.

Present Teachings

Today's teachings insist that this concept of the free will of man began in the garden with Adam and the woman. It's been explained how God had commanded Adam not to eat of the tree of good and evil, in the midst of the garden, how they ate of it anyway after the serpent tricked the woman. How she looked into the tree and ate then gave it to Adam who was with her and he did eat. There is a belief that nothing happened until Adam ate because he was in charge. They go on to say God got angry because Adam and the woman had made a conscious decision to disobey him and eat from the tree. It is believed that this was the first example of a man having free will. Based on present teaching, Adam and the woman had a God-given right to agree or disagree with God as they saw fit. Now, the question is, "When did God give them this 'free will'?" Was it when he blew his Spirit into the Living Soul, or right before Adam ate? It had to be some time between the blowing of the Spirit and them eating the fruit. When do you think it happened? However, I cannot find any scriptural proof to back up this claim. Therefore, the question is, "the free will of man," where did it come from, and who does it benefit? I found it interesting that after searching the Scriptures (I googled it too) there are no Scriptures indicating that God ever said or indicated to the man that he could rebel against him (God) and that he (God) was okay with that. In fact, God declared that they must surely die. Did he change his mind and went back on his word? Was he only talking about a spiritual death? In this case, the separation of Adam's spirit from his body was impossible because to remove his Spirit would have left the body lifeless, because the blood was not the life force at the time. Wait a minute, there may be a place in the Scriptures that indicated that the eating was going to take place. We find in Genesis 2:17 that God made a very interesting statement. He said, "But of the tree of the knowledge of good and evil, thou shalt not eat of it: for in the day that thou eatest thereof thou shalt surely die." Now, "In the day that thou eatest thereof" is a powerful statement, being that "in a day" is a point in time. In this case, the start and/or finishing of something. Also, when God speaks a thing, it must come true. Intriguing, is it not? Anyway, James 2:26 tells us, "For as the body without the spirit is dead, so faith without works is dead also." Nowhere in the scriptures has this ever happened to Adam. More on this later in the narrative. There are two scriptures that mention the phrase "will of man"; they are:

> But as many as received him, to them he gave the power to become the sons of God, even to them that believe on his name: Which were born, not of blood, nor of the will of the flesh, nor of the *will of man*, but of God. (John 1:12–13; emphasis mine)

> For the prophecy, came not in old time by the *will of man*: but holy men of God spake as they were moved by the Holy Ghost. (2 Pet. 1:22; emphasis mine)

Neither one of these scriptures shines a good light on the "will of man." Being that (in my view) there is no scriptural evidence as to a "free will" of man or that it has any divine power associated with it. I concluded that the only "will" we have is the will of the one we follow. Therefore, those who follow mammon (riches) serve his will (John 8:44). A clearer understanding of this comes from 2 Corinthians 4:4, where we are taught that the devil is the god of this world, unto those who minds he has blinded, those who do not believe (unbelievers). My understanding is that the only "will" a believer has is the "will" of God. Mark 3:35 states that "For who shall do the will of God, the same is my brother, and my sister and mother." We find in Acts 13:36 that David served his generation by the "will of God" before he died. Finally, the narrative on the "free will of man" is one that is covered in evil and missing the mark. In Matthew 6:24, it talks about the two masters. One is God and the other being mammon. Our present-day teaching dictates that Satan is a master. However, the scriptures say that mammon is a master. *Strong's Concordance* G3226 identifies mammon as being treasure, riches, and wealth that is personified. The dictionary says that mammon is "a personification of riches as an evil spirit or deity." Personification is the placing of "attributes of [human nature or characteristics] on animals, inanimate objects, or abstract notions, especially as a rhetorical figure." Therefore, the will of man can only manifest when there is a focus on getting things and stuff. This action produces a love that is addictive to self-worth and not of God but of the world. In 1 John 2:16 it states that "For all that is in the world, the lust of the flesh, and the lust of the eyes, and the pride of life, is not of the Father, but is of the world." You cannot serve two masters.

However, I decided to go back and review what happened in the beginning with Adam and the woman to see what type of supposition I could come up with. The conclusion of this matter will continue later in the narrative. But until then, let us continue with "Is the doctrine you are being taught the true Gospel of our Lord Jesus, the Christ our God, or not?" Many in the pulpit, unknowingly or knowingly, have become self-serving businesspersons who *went* rather than was being *sent*. Many of them teach Old Testament theology, which highlights the disobedience, rejections, and the unbelief that the children of Israel had toward God. Then they attempt to apply that theology onto New Testament believers. These concepts and precepts are so far from being accurate. It leads us to a philosophy of expectation. This philosophy would have us believe that Jesus deals with us (believers) the same way he deals with sinners (unbelievers). Let us look at this: Paul said, "Let this mind be in you that was in Christ Jesus." Can we conclude that if we, New Testament saints, have the mind of Christ, then we have pleased the Father and do not expect him to do what he already has done? Let us take a look and see how we please God. In Hebrews 11:5, we find Enoch, who was the seventh from Adam (the seventh generation, three hundred years after Adam left the garden), pleasing God because of his testimony. His testimony was that he believed and trusted God to take care of him. Proverbs 3:5 says, "Trust in the Lord with all thine heart and lean not unto thine own understanding. In all thy ways acknowledge him, and he shall direct thy path." Therefore, to have the mind of Christ is to please God by knowing that he will take good care of us regardless of the situation or circumstances. Paul goes on to say Christ did not think it was robbery to be equal with God but "was made in the likeness of men" in order to be obedient to the death on the cross. We must understand that Christ never stopped being God but took on the appearance of a man in order not to shock the people with his presence. In Exodus 33:20–23, God tells Moses that no man can see his face and live. Placing Moses behind a rock, he showed him only his back parts. If Christ would have come in his perfect appearance, the people could not have withstood it. Exodus 20:20 indicates that the people were afraid of God even talking to them directly, for fear of death. The book of 1 John indicates that when Christ comes again, we will be just like him. That appearance, which is like his, happened to him before the foundation of the world.

Christology vs. Theology

Trying to teach New Testament Christology (Jesus) using Old Testament theology (God) is a very tricky thing to do, because the precepts are the same in some aspects yet very different in others. That is because the Old was based on works, rejections, and unbelief, while the New is based on grace, acceptance, and belief. To be clear, the Old focused on disobedience while the new focus is on obedience. There are many in the congregation that are just followers never coming to the truth of the Scriptures. They say amen, bear witness, wave their hands, and tell their neighbor whatever they are told by the person speaking, like robots, rarely knowing what the person is saying or what they mean. Another misleading doctrine is that Satan has the ability to overrule Jesus's commands. The truth is that he can only rule over those who do not believe (unbelievers); this is according to 2 Corinthians 4. In addition, Satan, who is said to be the god of this world, can rule over them, so they cannot have the light of Christ shine on them and God would have to save them. A question arises to me: Are those the ones God turned over to a reprobate mind (Rom. 1:28)? In 1 Thessalonians 2:11, God is the one that gave them a strong delusion that they should believe a lie. The lie was that they knew better than God what they needed to feel good. Therefore, it is God, not Satan, that blinded their minds; interesting.

The Rulership of Satan

Question: When we talk about Satan doing this or that, are we actually talking about his seed, Cain, and his descendants (1 John 3)? You see, the descendants of Cain are vagabonds and fugitives, as their father was (Gen. 4:14). They are known as the children of disobedience or the sons and daughters of men (*Strong's Concordance*, H120).

Also, we are no longer under the law of sin and death but are under the law of life in Christ Jesus. James 4:5–10 talks to us about dealing with the devil. He says, "Do ye think that the scripture saith in vain, The spirit that dwelleth in us lusteth to envy? But he giveth more grace. Wherefore he saith, God resisteth the proud, but giveth grace unto the humble. Submit yourselves therefore to God. Resist the devil, and he will flee from you." We find here that we have the grace of God because of our humbleness, and because of that grace, we can resist the devil, and he has no choice but to flee. The process of being humble is found in Ephesians 1:13, that says, "In whom ye also trusted, after that ye heard the word of truth, the gospel of your salvation: in whom also after that ye believed, ye were sealed with that holy Spirit of promise." The outline here is to first hear, then trust, and believed. Then God seals you with the Holy Spirit. The "hearing" here is not from a person but from God who calls us (1 Peter 2:9). "Trusted" (G4276) is a pass tenth word, which means "to hope before." Now that hope comes from his faith (Hebrews 11:1). To "believe" (G4102) is to "relating to God, the conviction that God exists and is the Creator and ruler of all things, the provider and bestower of eternal salvation through Christ. Relating to Christ, a strong and welcome conviction or belief that Jesus is the Messiah, through whom we obtain eternal salvation in the kingdom of God." And finally, to be "sealed" (G4972) is the most important of all these words, for it means "to set a seal upon, mark with a seal, to seal, for security from Satan." Since things sealed up are concealed (as the contents of a letter), to hide, keep in silence, keep secret, (Colossians 3:3), this tells me that Satan has no authority over anything. To close this notion of Satan's control over us, the writer of 1 John states that if your heart (spirit) condemns you, God (Jesus) is greater than your heart (spirit) and knows all. The message here is that Satan brings sin, sin brings condemnation, and condemnation brings death (separation from God). This writer further informs us that no condemnation means our confidence toward God (Jesus) is intact and he will never leave us nor forsake us. Finally, Satan (Lucifer), being an angel is a heavenly being. I have found nowhere in the Bible where he has given residency or caretaker duties over the earth by God. The only one God gave caretaker duties over the earth was the Living Soul. Therefore, Satan has no authority or power over the earth and is an undocumented resident, an illegal alien, and a convict with a death sentence on his head. Jude 1:9 tell us this: "Yet Michael the archangel, when contending with the devil he disputed about the body of Moses, durst not bring against him a railing accusation, but said, The Lord rebuke thee. Our job is to only remind him what God has already done to him"

Another aspect of this Satan going to get you doctrine is that the book of Romans tells us that there is no condemnation upon those who love the Lord and called for his purpose.

Another strictly taught doctrine within primarily the charismatic movement is the healing ministries. The claim is that because of their close relationship with God, he works through them via the Holy Spirit to heal the sick, raise the dead, control the elements, etc. This attitude of miraculous healing and element manipulation comes from several conjectures and omissions between what Jesus and others said and what they did. Within this movement, there is a strong need to show evidence that you have the power, which is speaking in a heavenly language. However, what I have noticed is that the first time something happens, they are the first ones to run for cover. If they get sick or injured, they run to the doctor. They do this after telling their members not to trust the doctor but just trust Jesus to heal you. Many times, they cry out to the Lord to fix this or that right after they have proclaimed they have been given all powers. They claim that they were given this power to finish the works of Jesus. The proclamation they can do these things comes from scriptures like Matthew 4:23, where Jesus went about healing all manner of sickness and disease, or Luke 4:40, where Jesus healed all those brought to him, and also, Acts 5:16, where the multitude got healed when Peter passed by. The classic scripture used is John 14:12, where Jesus says, "Verily, verily, I say unto you, He that believeth on me, the works that I do shall he do also; and greater works than these shall he do; because I go unto my Father." This is the primary evidence use to declare that they have all the abilities of Jesus. However, the key phrase is "the work that I do he do also." What then are the works of Jesus? We find that Jesus's mission was to save his people from their sins by proclaiming the kingdom of God was at hand (accessible to his chosen). The acts he did were the results of being in the kingdom of God. Jesus was showing his people what it meant to be in the kingdom of God. The objective was for them to accept him for who he was and not what he did. Jesus confirmed this in John 6 when talking to the disciples. This is the conversation, "Then said they unto him, 'What shall we do, that we might work the works of God?' Jesus answered and said unto them, 'This is the work of God, that ye believe on him whom he hath sent.' They said therefore unto him, 'What sign shewest thou then, that we may see, and believe thee? What dost thou work?'" As he continued the conversation, we will understand the true works of God. Jesus then said to them, "All that the Father giveth me shall come to me; and him that cometh to me I will in no wise cast out. For I came down from heaven, not to do mine own will, but the will of him that sent me. And this is the Father's will which hath sent me, that of all which he hath given me I should lose nothing, but should raise it up again at the last day. And this is the will of him that sent me, that every one which seeth the Son, and believeth on him, may have everlasting life: and I will raise him up at the last day." This is a direct reference to John 17, where he states he had lost none given him. An important thing Jesus said to the seventy was this, "Notwithstanding in this rejoice not, that the spirits are subject unto you; but rather rejoice, because your names are written in heaven." Therefore, we are to rejoice about who and whose we are and not on what we can do. There many other scriptures that dictate that if Jesus or one of the apostles did this or that, then they can do it too.

In Romans 9:15–16, God declares, "I will have mercy on whom I will have mercy, and I will have compassion on whom I will have compassion. So then it is not of him that willeth, nor of him that runneth, but of God that sheweth mercy." I think claiming to have God's power to do the things of God is a very dangerous thing to do. My perspective only.

Review

This leads us back to the question, "Is the doctrine we are being taught the true Gospel of Christ?" In the scriptures, we are told that in the last days there will be many out to deceive the elect. Their objective is to make merchandise of us. We are told they will come as ministers of righteousness and that they will take captive many with subtle speak, just as the serpent did to the woman. Well then, ask yourself that question: Am I sure the doctrine being preached to me is the true Gospel, or is it another gospel? Think about it; deception is a subtle thing that can have eternal consequences.

Remember this: The Lord has chosen you and not you that chose him. His love toward us is based on who you are in his sight. It is not that you know him but rather that he knows you (Gal. 4:9). Finally, Paul says in 1 Timothy, "Study to show yourself approved, a workman able to rightly divide the word of God."

WHY DOES THIS MATTER?

Who Is Adam?

Before we dive into understanding this question, the reader must check or review their narrative about the nature of man. You see, the primary narrative that we are taught is that man is a fallen creature in need of redemption, that he gave his position and status up because of disobedience. Further, there is an understanding that the name Adam is connected in some way to the phrase "sinful flesh." I must caution you to truly review the substance of this narrative; you must realize that the natures of good and evil refer to the natures of Cain (the unrighteous one) and Abel (the righteous one). Therefore, this narrative has separated the cultural line of Cain from the cultural line of Abel (Seth, Gen. 4:25). To use natural analysis, it is like a train track. The train travels on a track that consists of two rails; although they are parallel, they never cross. This is how the nature of man is; good and evil runs parallel, but they never cross. Again, before going further, review your narrative about the nature of man. Now, let us go on. And may God bless.

Recently I was asked this question while discussing some aspects of our Christian belief. This question generated itself from a conversation about Jesus the Christ. For many years, we have been taught only the deity, the supernatural nature of Jesus with little or no interest in his humanity, his natural nature. The reason we do not look into his humanity is that we equate it to the flesh. Our belief about the flesh is that there is no good thing that comes out of it. We know that his deity came from God Almighty, but where did his humanity come from? I asked myself this question and I am asking you now: Is Jesus's deity linked to his humanity? I think, in order to look into his human nature, we will find where his earthly nature actually came from and how it relates to his deity.

Our current teaching dictates he was both 100 percent human (flesh), his weak nature, and 100 percent God (Spirit), his strong nature. We are further taught he existed as the "Word" with God at the beginning of creation. Was he in the spirit or flesh? Well then, if he was in the spirit, when did Jesus change to a fleshly man? Now, why, in Genesis 2:5, was there no man (human) to till (take care of) the ground of the earth? We see that the *Living Soul* which God blew his Spirit (himself) into (John 4:24) was formed out of the ground, outside of the garden, and he became the incarnation (manifestation) of God, his embodiment, that had a purpose. A very important question presents itself here. That question is, "How much of God's Spirit did he blow into the Living Soul?" Was it 10%, 25%, 50%, or 100%? Just asking. His purpose was to bring order to the chaotic earth, which was void and without form. Presently, it is taught that God created man for his pleasure, and man's purpose is to please and serve God. I find no mention of this teaching in the forming of the man outside of the garden. Anyway. He was to accomplice this by cultivating the environment into the nature of God. Now, when God formed the Living Soul out of the ground and blew the breath of life in him, he, the Living Soul, became full of God's life. The Living Soul was injected with the full nature of God. In Isaiah 45:7, we find God identifying who he is and what he did at creation: "I form the light, and create darkness: I make peace, and *create evil*: I the Lord do all these things" (emphasis mine). Do you think God withheld any of these attributes of his nature from the Living Soul? How could he? Because they were one ("And the glory which thou gavest me I have given them; that they may be one, even as we *are one*" [John 17:22; emphasis mine]). To be the fullest of God is to be in the right standing with God. The question is, who could separate the Living Soul from God (Rom. 8:35–39)? We are also told in Colossians 2:8–11, to

> Beware lest any man spoils you through philosophy and vain deceit, after the tradition of men, after the rudiments of the world, and not

> after Christ. For in him dwelleth all the fulness of
> the Godhead bodily. And ye are complete in him,
> which is the head of all principality and power: In
> whom also ye are circumcised with the circumci-
> sion made without hands, in putting off the body of
> the sins of the flesh, by the circumcision of Christ.

Therefore, who or whatever God is, the Living Soul must be the same. To me, the keyword here is "beware." *Strong's Concordance* G991 shows that beware means "metaph; to see with the mind's eye; to have (the power of) understanding; examine." However, the *Concordance's* meaning in Hebrew H8104 is this, "to keep, guard, protect, save life; watch, watchman." Well, is this an option? I digress, sorry.

Therefore, everything God knew the Living Soul knew, and everything God could do the Living Soul could do also. This was verified by Jesus in John 8:28 when he stated that "…and I do nothing of myself; but as my Father hath taught me…." A question that goes along with this is, "When and how was Jesus taught the things of the Father?"

What then is a living soul? A living soul is a speaking spirit that is contained within a container. In this case, the container consisted of the elements from the ground from which he was formed, while his animation was by the Spirit of God that was within him. The psalmist asked the question of "What is man?" and others of old asked the same question (Job 7:17; Ps. 8:4 and 144:3). The answer to this question indicates that this man (the Living Soul) was someone that was already in existence and yet someone who was to come (Rom, 5:12–14, 1 Tim. 2:14, and Gen. 5:2). In Hebrews 2:6, we find a testimony from the past, which indicates that this person existed from the beginning, and God was mindful of him and thought highly of him. However, there is no indication that God ever thought less of him or cast him away at any time. Now, the forming of the Living Soul, from the ground outside of the garden, connected him to the earth and all its environments and elements. This was an exceptional act by God, in that it allowed him to establish a colony (kingdom) on Earth that was in the midst of chaos. The unique thing about the Living Soul was that he is not only a speaking spirit enclosed in the container of the earth, but he is also the complete man that God needed and wanted. This is because this allowed him to fulfill his earthly duties as God's representative (caretaker). Therefore, God Almighty, who is outside of time and space (John 4:24), made himself a visible (physical) representative, (an ambassador [2 Cor. 5:20]), which was able to totally connect with his earthly environments and elements and with God at the same time. In addition, he gave him (Man) rule over all the host of things, which he (God) had previously spoken into existence. Here I must interject something. We are taught that man is a three-part being—body, soul, and spirit. We have further been taught that the body houses the spirit and the soul. And they (Spirit and soul) war with each other for control of our emotions and feelings. *Strong's Concordance* H5315 informs us that "soul" means "that which breathes, the breathing substance or being," soul, "the inner being of man." Therefore, my understanding is that the Spirit of God is what he (God) blew into the Man that made him (the Man) a living soul, and the living soul belongs to and is controlled by God. It must be noted that in Matthew 10:28, this warning is given, "And fear not them which kill the body, but are not able to kill the soul: but rather fear him which is able to destroy both soul and body in hell." Here, there is no mention of humans being a three-part creature. Only body and soul.

The Command and the Results

Another exceptional thing that God did in Genesis 2:5–7, after forming the Living Soul outside of the garden, he then planted a garden. Now, there's something very interesting about this garden that God planted eastward in Eden. It is a basic understanding that the word "eastward" is referring to a location or direction; however, *Strong's Concordance* H6924 indicate that this word has other intriguing meanings which are "antiquity, that which is before, aforetime, from the front or east, in front, mount of the East, ancient time, aforetime, ancient, from of old, earliest time, anciently, of old (adverb), and beginning." I would like to focus on the meaning of "ancient time." Could it be that God placed the Living Soul somewhere in a time before? An aforetime? Okay, let us continue. Within the garden, he established the tree of life and the tree of the knowledge of good and evil, within the midst of it. Noting here that God, right after he put the Living Soul in the garden, he then formed everything he had created from the ground of the garden. This was a duplication of everything he had already previously spoken into existence, outside of the garden. A question: what then was the purpose of the garden and the duplication of his spoken creation? Well, it could have been a place to protect the Living Soul from the outside conditions and environment, or it could have been a place of safety for the Living Soul to train and learn the things of God, by God without interruptions, until it was time to assume his purpose (position) of tilling, taking care of, the outside ground (Gen. 2:5). Another question is, what then was the purpose of the trees in the midst of the garden? (Note, they were not mentioned in Genesis 1:30.) Could they had been placed there as a test? We know what the consequences were for eating from the tree of the knowledge of good and evil. The results were that their eyes would be opened to good and evil. We also know the consequences if they had eaten from the tree of life (Gen. 3:22). They would have stayed in the garden forever.

At this point, Genesis tells us the creatures that were duplicated were then presented before the Living Soul, so he could call its name. Could this have been the way God confirmed his spiritual link between him and the Living Soul? You see, the Living Soul called the creatures by its name, thereby establishing ownership over all the creations God had created. It must be noted that a declaration of ownership is based on the owner establishing his property's name, which identified its owner (Gen. 1:28). Now, to have ownership of something means to be responsible for and to it at all cost. Therefore, the Living Soul (that God formed from the ground) became the King (Chief Authority, the Messiah, the Christ, and the Son of God) over his environment (the colony) by accepting responsibility for it. In addition, because he had the Spirit of God within him, he was linked to God, as his priest (mediator) of the Most High God. Therefore, he (the Living Soul) is the King of kings and Lord of lords (Rev. 17:14) on the earth. That means (to me), the Living Soul is the master of

Earth's elements and environments and could bend them to his will as necessary. This is why Jesus could command the environment and elements in Mark 4:30 when he rebuked the wind and told the sea to have peace and be still, and they obeyed. The Living Soul is the same yesterday, today, and forever (Heb. 13:8). This narrative is confirmed in John 1:3, when it was said, "All things were made by him; and without him was not anything made that was made."

Jesus and the Living Soul

How then is Jesus tied to the living soul, who was formed from the ground at the beginning? Let us see, it is written in 1 Corinthians 15:45 that the first man (Adam) was made a living soul. The process of him being made a living soul is based on having the Spirit of God in him. The Spirit of God, which is the spirit of truth (John 16:13), that guides us to all truth. The first man (living soul) had this happen to him when God blew his Spirit into his earthly form at the beginning. Now, the last man (Adam) was made a quickening spirit (a living soul). This happened when he completed his mission of destroying the works of the devil (1 John 3:8) then yielding up the ghost (Matt. 27:50 and Heb. 5:8–10). It must be understood that both the man the living soul and the man the quickening spirit were both *made* from and contained the same substances, the ground of the earth and the Holy Spirit of God. Both were flesh and bone, animated by the Spirit of God (Gen. 2:23 and Luke 24:39). Luke 3:22–38 tells us that Jesus is a direct descendant of the man from the ground. They both are eternally married to the church (Eph. 5:25–32 and Gen. 2:21–24). In John 10:30, Jesus declared that "I and my Father are One." In addition, in Romans 5:14, Paul tells us that Adam "…is the figure of him that was to come" (Jesus).

Why then does this matter? Well, Jesus' ascendants affected their environment and influenced many into the ways of God Almighty. Also, it is important to note that in Exodus 6:3, Psalm 83:18, and Isaiah 12:2 and 26:4 (KJV), Abraham, Isaac, and Jacob's God was named Jehovah the Existing One (*Strong's Concordance*, H3068). Further, we understand that the title Lord belongs to Jehovah or

Jesus (*Strong's Concordance*, G2960). The holy Scriptures concludes that Jehovah operated as Israel's God on earth and in the heavenly realm as the living spirit. The Hebrews knew him as the God of war (Exodus 15:3) that protected Israel from the other gods. Psalm 136:2 informs us that the God of Israel became known as the God of gods.

We are taught that our Christian precepts come from father Abraham, who is a descendant of Shem, a descendant of Noah, a descendant of Enoch, and a descendant of Seth (who replaced Abel, Gen. 4:25–26) and is the son of the man (Adam, the living soul), the son of God (Luke 3:34–38). Why does it matter? Well, we cannot know who we are unless we know who is the fullest of Godhead bodily (Col. 2:8–10). The one thing God wants us to know is who and whose we are (Luke 15:17). For in him (Christ) we have life and are hidden in God (Col. 3:3).

The Righteousness of God

Why does this matter? Well, the teachings of today are primarily focused on what humans need to do in order to get into a right standing (righteous status) with God. This teaching is based on the precept there is none who is righteous. We are taught that in order to become righteous, we must do this or that, and because we do this or that, God has no choice but to bless us. The conventional saying is "that if he did it for me, he will do it for you." I cannot find in the Scriptures where God (who is outside of time and space) is getting ready to do what he has already done, both in and outside of your life (James 4:11–12, The Message). It must be noted that in the New Testament that God deals with us as individuals and not as a corporate body as he did with the children of Israel. Remember in John3:16, we are told that "whosoever believe," and Jesus said in John 17 that he had lost none that was given him. These are acts about dealing with individuals. We are taught, all we need to do is keep following the rules as outlined, and God is getting ready to bless us. However, we will find that the original use of the word is wrapped in the context of the first man who was full of the Holy Spirit of God (*Strong's Concordance*, H121). In Genesis 2:1, we find God was surveying the earth, the heavens, and all the hosts of them and declared all finished and very good. After that, he rested; this was the seventh day. Genesis 2:5 indicates that God had not caused it to rain and there was no man to till the ground. It goes on in verse 6 to say that God caused a mist from the earth that watered the face of the ground; verse 7 shows the forming of the man out of the ground. In addition, it is important to note that this particular man was unique in that God blew his Spirit in him (he did not do this to any other of his creatures). God then gave the form a name called Adam (the red earth [*Strong's Concordance*, G76, H121, the first man]). The importance of this is that H120 refers to human beings as in many, while H121 refers to one specific person. Paul tells us in Galatians 3:16 that "now to Abraham and his seed were the promises made. He saith not, And to seeds, as of many; but as of one, And to thy seed, which is Christ."

The Two become One; Christ and the Church

Now, after God had formed the man from the ground outside of the garden, he placed him in the garden and had him call the names of all that God had created, then God declared that Adam needed a helpmeet (*Strong's Concordance*, H5828; helper, aid, assistant). The primitive root word for *helper* is *aw-zar* (*Strong's Concordance*, H5826), which means to surround, as in protect. The importance of this is that Adam needed someone like him to surround (protect) and assist him while he learned to take care of the garden in order to take care of the ground outside of the garden. In other words, he required a gatekeeper to guard and take care of him while he learned to take care of the garden. We find in Genesis 2:20 that there was not a suitable helpmeet (aide) among the present creatures for Adam. That someone needed to have the same position in order to assist Adam in being the keeper of God's creation. Therefore, God decided that the only place to find an acceptable helpmeet was on the inside of Adam (verses 21–22). He knew that by coming out of Adam, this person would be an excellent assistant, because she would be environmentally linked to him. However, she did not have the status (connection) with God that Adam had, because she did not have God's Spirit within her. After a successful operation, God brought the helpmeet to Adam for him to call her name. In addition, Genesis 2:23 stated that Adam called her name wo-man, meaning "out of man" (Adam from Adam). Afterward, Adam laid down some rules concerning his relationship with the wo-man, which came out of him. The basic rule as laid out in verse 24 is, "…and they shall be one flesh"; "bone of my bone and flesh of my flesh" (verse 23). This indicates that each had a role to perform; for the failure or success of one had an impact on the other. It must be noted that in Genesis 5:2, God declares that he called *their* name Adam. This could be because the two was one. Finally, they both had the position of keepers of all God had created but not the same status as the incarnate of God. It must be noted here that a very important thing happened here. God reached inside of Adam and pull the woman out. The Greek word for this action is *ekklesia* (*Strong's Concordance*, G1577). This is a compound word coming from *Strong's Concordance* (G1537—*ek*, which is to be from or out; and G2564—*kaleo*, which is to call, invite, or to receive the name of). Why does this matter? Well, you see, the word *ekklesia* is the Greek word for *church*. You see, when God pulled the woman out of Adam, he was bringing the church into existence; the church, which is the keeper of the promise (Jesus).

The Plan

Well then, why does this matter? We know that all of this is within the master plan of God. In Isaiah 46:10–12 is when God declared to the transgressors (those that were unrighteous) that the end was declared from the beginning. Isaiah 48:3–5 indicates that the former things were declared from the beginning and they were declared at the beginning to thee (the house of Jacob, the obstinate ones). God stated that all the things he declared came to pass.

Now, in Ephesians 5, Paul tells us in verse 25 that something happened for which Christ (the Living Soul, the incarnate of God) had to give himself (sacrifice) for it (the church). The question in my mind is, when did the church do something that Christ had to give himself (sacrifice) for it? We know that the church was activated by Jesus (Matt. 16:18) and manifested in Acts after his departure. Maybe there is something you can think of that the church did that Christ had to sacrifice himself for. Nothing, okay? Well, if we read on in Ephesians 5, we find in verses 28–32 that Paul is referring to something at the beginning when the two shall be one flesh (verse 31). Wait a minute, isn't this the same thing Adam said about the woman in Genesis 2:23–24? "… and they shall be one flesh." In order to explore what Paul was leading up to concerning the great mystery of Christ and the church, we must go to the beginning when Adam declared the woman as his wife (Gen. 2:24). As a note: God had declared that he is married to Israel (Jer. 3:14). While in Revelation 21, we find that the new Jerusalem is prepared as the bride for the Lamb (Christ, the incarnate of God). Now then, how does this link to the beginning?

Before we continue, there must be some background information set forward. In Luke 10:18, Jesus makes a statement that he saw Satan fall from heaven. Focusing on the context of this statement, the question arises about "where was Jesus when he saw this?" It is the belief of some that this was at the beginning when he was on earth as the incarnation of God (Living Soul) or in heaven as the male child of the woman which was place safely on the throne of God that hid him from the dragon (Rev. 12:1–6). This was during the time of the great war in heaven (verses 7–9). These things possibly happened before Adam (the living soul) was formed out the ground. You can determine which of these hypotheses (if either) you want to believe. The focus here is on the fact that Satan was cast to the earth in disgrace. The indications in both Isaiah and Revelation are that Satan (Lucifer) was cast down to the earth among the people on earth as a prisoner. This is noted in Revelation 12:12 when the hosts of heaven warned the "…inhabiters of the earth that the dragon was coming with great wrath in the persecution of the woman that birthed the man-child." Isaiah 14:12–20 gives us a look at what happened to Lucifer when he was cast down from heaven to the earth after the war in heaven. Many have declared this is Israel, which brought forth Jesus the Christ (the incarnation of God). However, I must caution that when the war in heaven happened, there was no Israel, because this happened in the beginning. We know Satan represents darkness, evil, and wickedness that covered the face of the earth in the beginning. A question is, "were these inhabitants on earth that the heavenly warned about the arrival of the dragon, the same ones the devil showed Jesus in the wilderness that he supposedly had control over? Do your research to answer this question. Now let us stay focused. In Genesis 3, a new creature enters into the picture, the serpent. This creature was considered more subtle than all the creatures God had created. Many times, we overlook this verse and the primary word in it. That word is *subtle*. In the *Strong's Concordance*, the word *subtil* is H6175. The meaning is cunning (usually in a bad sense): crafty, prudent. The dictionary added another word as being related; that word is *cunning*. To be cunning is to have knowledge of something, and with that knowledge comes understanding (Prov. 4:7). Understanding in this verse is the *Strong's Concordance* H998, which is to have wisdom, knowledge, and meaning. The root word for *understanding* is *Strong's Concordance* H995, which is identified as *biyn*, which is "to discern, understand, consider; to perceive, know (with the mind); to observe, mark, give heed to, distinguish, consider; to have discernment, insight, intelligent, discreet." One of the *Strong's Concordance* phrases of the word is "be cunning." Therefore, because the serpent was the most *subtil* (cunning) of all of God's spoken creations, he had knowledge and understanding of things that the other creatures did not have. This made him an excellent candidate for Satan to use to spread discord. In Genesis 3, we find the serpent asking the woman a question. This question included information that the serpent knew that no other creature knew including the woman who had no connection to the knowledge and wisdom of God. In relation to Genesis 1:29, God did tell the man that he could eat from every tree that yielded seed could be meat to eat. In addition, he (Satan) did tell the woman in verse 3 that "God doth know that in the day they ate, their eyes would be open." Which raises the question of, did God want their eyes open to all things or not? This raises another question of, which came first, the trees of the earth (verse 29) or the trees in the midst of the garden (Gen. 2:9)? Did the serpent trick (deceive) the woman by talking about the trees outside of the garden while knowing she only knew about the trees within the garden? Another interesting thought is, did she act on what the serpent said or what she saw (Gen. 3:6)? Could it be that she was deceived by what she saw rather than what she heard (1 Tim. 2:14)? Oh well, regardless of the reason, it is all a part of God's master plan, is it not? Because of her action, her purpose changed from co-keeper of creation, when she ate. Genesis 3 goes on to identify that she gave the fruit to her husband that was with her and he ate. A question here is, if Adam was right next to her, why didn't the serpent engage in a conversation with him? Anyway, there are several opinions here; one is that Adam should have stepped in and confronted the serpent and reminded the woman of her duties. Another opinion dictates that Adam should not have eaten and informed God what the woman had done. Because there are no references as to either of these opinions, let's just move on. Excuse me, to return to the question of "What did the Church do that Christ had to sacrifice himself for?" take a look at 2 Timothy 2:14: "And Adam was not deceived, but the woman being deceived was in the transgression." *Strong's Concordance* G3847 says "transgression" is "a disregarding, violating." The root word G3845 indicates it to mean "to overstep, neglect, violate, transgress, so to go past as to turn aside from, to depart, leave, be turned from, one who abandons his trust." You see, when she looked into the tree, she disregarded all she knew and had been told. Now, when Adam ate the fruit, he sacrificed himself for her (the Church) because she had transgressed him and needed a savior.

The Cause and Effect

Now, the consequence of them eating was that their eyes were opened. The question then is, their eyes were opened to what? The general consensus is that their eyes were opened to their nakedness; this led to their shame. There is an understanding that after their eyes were opened, they were afraid. What then were they afraid of? Could it have been of the exposure of eating from the forbidden trees, were they ashamed of what they had lost, or was it the fear of the wrath of God for their disobedience? Note, the question God asked Adam about his location was not a question of interrogation but one of reve-lation. The revelation was unto Adam for he had just been downloaded with all the information and experiences of God. You do remember that he is the living soul and had the hard drive of the Holy Spirit in him. This is an indication that he now understood that he had a violation against him. The violation of being aware of his nakedness and what it meant. In fact, the answer to God's question to Adam about where he was indicates that their violation had been exposed. It is further indicated that the exposure of their nakedness generated the spirit of fear, condemnation, and flight from God's punishment that was at hand. However, we see that God's question about Adam's location was directed at Adam and not his wife. As we continue with this aspect of the narrative, the general consensus is that Adam blamed the woman. God pronounced judgment on Adam and the woman and drove them out of the garden for their disobedience and bringing sin into the world. The final commonly held opinion to this narrative is that they had disobedient children; then the flood came. This led to the belief that man fell from something, which started the narrative called the "Fall of Man," the time sinful flesh entered the world.

Why does all this matter? Well, if we take a closer look at Genesis 3:13–21—the area of this book that is not explored enough—here we find God begin to interrogate the subjects before him. After the confession of Adam that he was afraid, naked, hid, and did eat, God asked the question, "Who told you that you were naked?" There is an important note here. The word naked in *Strong's Concordance* has two separate designations. One is H6174, which is to be "bare." This one is designated as being without shame (Genesis 2:25). The other one is H5903, which is "nakedness," (Genesis 3:7). However, the root word is very enlightening for it is H6191, which means "to be subtle, be shrewd, be crafty, beware, take crafty counsel, be prudent, to be crafty, be subtle, be or become shrewd." The enlightening thing is that this is the same designation given to the subtle serpent (Genesis 3:1). Could this mean that the living soul had become even more subtle than the serpent and all other creations? Okay, let's continue. This exchange is interesting in that the only one Adam had contact with was the woman. Therefore, the only possible person or thing that he had a relationship with was the woman. In addition, that was the answer that Adam gave God, the woman you gave me. Was that the truth or not? He went on to answer the second part of God's question: had he eaten from the tree of good and evil? His answer was yes, he did. Now, at this juncture, we are taught that Adam blamed the woman for his disobedience; however, he was only answering the questions that God had asked. How would you have responded?

Next, God interrogated the woman by asking her, "What have you done?" Her response was the serpent beguiled her and she ate. But if we look closer, we find that the serpent first influenced her to look at the content of the tree. She found it to be good for food, pleasant to the eye, and could make one wise. Her eating of the tree was solely based on what she saw in the tree. The question, if you believe all the things that happened so far is a part of God's plan, is then what did she do wrong? So what is it that the serpent (Satan) wanted from the woman? We will come to that later.

We know that God did not interrogate the serpent but passed judgment on him. It is an understanding that Satan was the main target from the beginning. A target from the pit for what he did in heaven (Rev. 12). The judgment God pronounced on the serpent is interesting and is broken into a three-part prophecy. The first part was that he was cursed beneath all creatures. *Strong's Concordance* H7043, to curse means to "appear trifling, be too trifling, be insignificant." The second part was that there be a war between the woman and the serpent. This indicates the constant conflict between good and evil. The third part of the prophecy was that the seed of the serpent (unrighteousness) would bruise the heel of the seed of the woman (righteousness), and the seed of the woman would bruise the head of the seed of the serpent. This prophecy by God opens up the answer to several questions. One being the war for control of man is between Satan and the woman. We see that is all throughout history, Satan has been trying to destroy the seed of the woman to get control of humanity while she has been protecting her seed until the right time so that humanity could be free. However, the reason the serpent initially came to the woman was twofold: one because he was rebelling against God and the other because he needed her to birth his evil seed (offspring) to counter God forming of the Living Soul. That was the only way God's prophecy of him could come to pass. Now, the question God asked the woman, "What have you done?" Well, she listened to the voice of another and consumed the seeds of the fruit (good and evil). Overall, she committed adultery. You see, when the serpent spoke to her and she responded, she accepted the words, "not surely die and be as gods," and saw the fullness of the world. In 1 John 2:16, we find that the things of the world are the same things she saw in the tree, "For all that is in the *world*, the lust of the flesh, and the lust of the eyes, and the pride of life, is not of the Father, but is of the *world*" (emphasis mine).

There is a note here; many have taught that the man and the woman were in the image of God at his creation, so based on our present-day teaching the woman was already like God. However, godhood was not imparted to the man until Genesis 3:22. Anyway!

The aforementioned action about adultery can be compared to the virgin birth in Luke 1:30–31, when the angel came to Mary and spoke the words saying not to fear that she had found favor with the Lord and would conceive a son; her response was that she had not known a man and how this could be. However, she accepted the words by saying, "Behold the handmaid of the Lord; be it unto me according to thy word. And the angel departed from her." The woman confirmed that she believed the serpent by looking into the tree and ate. Just as Mary received and reacted to the words of the angel, she (the woman) received and reacted to the words spoken to her by the serpent.

Judgments and Punishments

Moving on to the judgment of the woman, after he had made the prophecy about the destiny of the seeds, God declared she would have great sorrow and sorrow in conception as she brings forth children. The last part of his judgment had to do with her relationship with her husband. She was told to desire (please) her husband, and he shall rule over her. The word "rule" in the *Strong's Concordance* is H4910, which means "to rule, have dominion, reign, to cause to rule, to exercise dominion." Has this changed?

As we move on to the judgment of Adam, we find some very interesting occurrences. The first one is that God says to him, "Because you hearkened [listened] unto the voice [words] of your wife and did eat." This is an indication that before Adam took the fruit from his wife and ate, they had a conversation. The question is, is there a reference as to what they talked about? Well, if we are of the understanding that Adam (the living soul) had the spirit of truth in him, the same spirit that connects you and me to God (Romans 8:26–27), then the natural answer would be he asked her the same question God asked her: "What is this you have done?" Now, at this point, Adam's decision was to take responsibility for her actions and eat. Remember, they were of one flesh and one bone, and what one did impacted the other for good or bad. In addition, Adam, by being the living soul, was duty-bound to protect all he was responsible for at all cost, even if it meant sacrificing himself.

Now, the question is, what would you have done? Would you have just run away and told God (who already knew what was going on) what the woman had done, or would you have taken responsibility for her actions and gave yourself for her?

As we continue on, the next thing God did was curse the ground that Adam was formed from; he did that for Adam's sake. Genesis 3:17 I find this interesting that he did not curse Adam directly but the ground. Why would God do such a thing? The ground had done nothing wrong. However, an important thing we have here is that he did it for Adam's sake. It must be noted that the word *sake* in the Hebrew *Strong's Concordance* is H5668, which means on account of, because, and in order to or in order that; however, the root word for *sake* means to pass over, cross, cross over, march over, and go over. We see by God cursing the ground for Adam's sake, he caused the curse harmlessly to pass over, cross over, or pass through him. Just as what happened with Noah and Ham in Genesis 9:24–27. It appears God did not curse him; therefore, he retained his status as (priest) and position as a (king) as God's representative on earth. If this were the case, then Adam did not lose his status as priest of the highest God (mediator) or his kingship over the earth (messiah). To show Adam still had status and position, he was able to rename his wife from woman (out of Adam) to Eve (life-giver). That name was given to her because her purpose changed from co-keeper of creation when she went into transgression (2 Tim. 2:14). In addition, she would be forever at war with the serpent (Rev. 12). Finally, because she gave birth to both Cain (unrighteousness), who was of the wicked one (1 John 3:12 and Zech. 5:5–9), and Abel, who was found righteous before God (Heb. 11:4). You see, Eve became the mother of all living because she gave birth to twins and all humans (both good and evil) come through her. In other words, two natures (righteous and unrighteous) pass through her line (1 Cor. 11:12). Today, the name Eve carries with it the title "mother of all living." Now, let us take a look at the ground that was cursed for Adam's sake. We noted that God placed a restriction on the ground's reproductive systems in relationship to Adam. The command given to the ground was that Adam had to work hard and long in order to retrieve its fruit. Note, this is not the same as the restrictions God put on the ground in relation to Cain (Gen. 4:12). Another overlooked note comes from Genesis 5:29 where at the birth of Noah, whose father Lamech stated that Noah would comfort their work and toil from the ground the Lord had cursed. You see, after the birth of Noah, those of his bloodline would not have to work hard to survive.

The Condemnation

The next part of this journey is one that is rarely or ever discussed. Many Christian leaders teach that man is a fallen creature and explain it with conjectures and omissions. Our teaching is that Adam brought sin into the world, therefore condemning all men to sin. The most used scripture for this teaching is Romans 3:23, "All have sinned." We will look at this later.

Demotion or Promotion

Now, the words that God spoke in Genesis 3:22 ring ever true or not. God spoke saying that the man (singular, H121) has become one of us (gods) knowing good and evil. Now, this verse creates a major problem for those of you who look at humankind as being totally sinful due to the transgression of Adam (the woman). But let us take a look back at Genesis 3:5. Here the serpent tells the woman that God knows. Well then, what is it that God knew? If we take a closer look at verse 22, God knew that in the day that they ate, they would become new creatures. Creatures that could discern both good and evil (Heb. 5:12). We find here that the discerning of good and evil is what makes one complete (full age, mature, perfect). Note, being perfect does not mean without error, but it means able to discern good and evil and choose the good. Isaiah 7:14–16 talks about the child of the virgin who had to learn to refuse the evil and choose the good (this is Jesus, right!). Therefore, if we remember that the man (Adam) is the living soul, the incarnation of God, who was God's representative on earth. In addition, we must understand that Adam did not lose his status as priest of the Most High God or his position as the mediator between God and all creation (messiah, king). All of this indicates (to me) that God was bestowing on the man his rightful title, which set him above all creation (Heb. 2:6–8).

This reflects back to the question above, "What is man?" Jesus himself stated in John 10:34–35 that the scriptures declared that "Ye are gods," and if God called them gods, then gods they are, for the scriptures cannot be broken. Let us look at what it means to be a god. Strong Concordance has several designations of the word "god," H430 means, rulers, judges, god, goddess while H410 means, God, the one true God, Jehovah. Confused? Do not be. You see, Jesus was quoting Psalms 82 when God was talking to the congregation of the mighty about their responsibilities as gods, the children of the Most High. Another interesting occurrence in this verse is the confession about eating from the tree of life. This is interesting because the eating of the tree of life would have enabled them to live in the garden forever in an incomplete state of being. Why is this important? Well, Adam's purpose was to take care of the ground of the earth for which he came from, not staying within the limits of the garden. This indicates that he would not have understood the darkness and the evil it presented outside the garden. The darkness that covered the face of the earth, the promoter of chaos and evil. Why does this matter? Well, the living soul's purpose of being is to destroy the works of the devil (1 John 3:8) and bring order to chaos. Now, we come to another important part of this journey, the leaving of the garden.

The primary teaching concerning this aspect of our journey is that the man was driven out of the garden because he ate the fruit given him, therefore violating God's commandment. However, verse 23 begins with the word *therefore*. Well, looking at the word *therefore*, we find it means "the result of something happening before." The event before the "therefore" was the statement of God about eating from the tree of life. So we can conclude that the "therefore" is referring to him not being able to eat from the tree and living forever. Why is this important? Well, if he had eaten from the tree of life, he would have gotten eternal life, then he would not have been able to do the things outlined in Genesis 1:28. Jesus cleared this up by saying that except a corn of wheat…dies, it cannot bring forth fruit (John 12:24). You see, except Adam died to self (sacrifice himself for someone or thing), he could not become all God wanted and needed him to be (a god), the ruler and judge of all God's earthly creation. The multiplicity of gods is stated in 1 Corinthians 8:5. There are those which are good and those which are evil gods. Moreover, they are known as mighty (Ps. 82) men of old, men of renowned (influencers) (Gen. 6:4). Now, before we venture into this understanding, let us finalize our look into Genesis 3 and moving on to Genesis 4. Looking back, we find something extraordinary happens right before God bestowed the man's title on him. In verse 21, God clothed them in coats of skins. There must be a special reason for God doing this. The basic teaching on the subject is unknown; maybe because of the complexity of the answer. However, let us take a closer look at what was said and how it fits with this narrative. Remember, what God says in the scriptures, he means; God is able to interpret himself. Verse 21 states, "… the Lord God make…," then that means the Lord God made. Any questions? Now, can we find a related verse somewhere to give us direction? In Revelations 13:8, we find that the Lamb was slain from the foundation of the world. The question now is when did the world begin? In *Strong's Concordance*, H2986 is the root word for world, the meaning being "to bring forth, lead forth and to bear along." Looking from this aspect of the word, it would indicate that some type of action brought the world forth. Could it be that the skins that God clothed them with were the skins of the Lamb slain from (the beginning of time) the foundation of the world? You do know that time began when Adam and his wife left the garden. It (time) started counting down from this point, heading to the ending, which is the complete defeat of Satan (Armageddon, Rev. 16:16). This being the case, Adam and his wife were clothed in the bloodstained skins of the Lamb (Jesus), the same thing that protects us from evil.

Well, if you are still here, that means you find this interesting on some level. Maybe you understand where I am coming from and want to see where I am going. Anyway, as long as you understand me, you do not need to accept what I am saying.

The Family

However, moving on to the beginning of the world after Adam and his wife had left the garden, we now are introduced to their two sons, Cain and Abel. In Genesis 4:1–2, we are told that Adam knowing (the act of reproduction) his wife. It must be noted that knowing her only happened once producing two children. The implication here is that Cain and Abel were twins. As we find, Cain and Abel had duties to perform. Cain took care of the field and Abel took care of the flock. Now, I believe that they had been taught how to please God with an offering. Who taught them that in the process of time to bring an offering to God? I just thought I would ask. Verse 4 tells us that two offerings were presented to God. One was accepted and the other one was not. Why then was one accepted and one rejected? Hebrews 9:22 dictates that without the shedding of blood, there can be no remission of sin. This word *remission* is extremely important. Strong Concordance (G863) tell us that to be remitted means (freedom; [figuratively] pardon:—deliverance, forgiveness, liberty, remission). Abel gave his firstling of the flock and of the fat; it was accepted by God as a blood sacrifice. Cain (who also knew the requirements) gave the fruit of the ground and was rejected. Why then was he rejected? We are taught that his offering was rejected because it was not his best. However, could it be that there was no shedding of blood? Why then would Cain (who knew what to do) did not get a firstling from Abel? How then do we know that Cain knew what to do? Well, God asked him in verse 7, if you do well, would not you be accepted? At this point, Cain was very angry with

God, so angry he went into a fit (chaos). Now, the question is, why and where did his anger come from?

Before looking into this, a question arises in my mind; how does God deal with man? The common understanding is that he deals with man according to what he does or does not do. Does he deal with man according to what he does or who and whose he is? My answer is, our relationship with God is based on who and whose we are. You see, the first thing God asked Cain was, "Why are you wroth (angry)?" God knew why; it was because of who he was and whose he was. In 1 John 3:11–13 it explains that Cain was of the wicked one…and his works were evil (unrighteous). Nowhere in the scriptures is Adam referred to as being the wicked one. You see, Cain was the physical offspring of Satan (the wicked one), the line which would bruise the heel of the woman offspring. In verse 7, we find that God gave Cain some important instructions. He pointed out that sin was waiting for him at the door but he (Cain) could rule over him (sin). We notice that the next act of Cain was to slay his brother. Now, our teaching indicates here that this shows that we have a free will to do or not to do. Therefore, my understanding is that we do or not do based on who and whose we are. Our decisions are controlled by our nature, righteous or unrighteous. I believe that a person's nature is either good or evil (but not both). In Matthew 7:18 Jesus tells us that a good tree cannot bear evil fruit and a corrupt tree (evil) can't bear good fruit. Is Jesus right or wrong? Can a man be both good and evil at the same time? In Proverbs 16:33, we are told this: "The lot is cast into the lap, but its every decision is from the Lord." Therefore, every decision we make is from God.

Moving on to the point where Cain killed Abel, we find God's judgment on Cain. The imposed judgments where he would be a fugitive (wander) and a vagabond (discontent) and the ground would not yield its strength. In other words, Jesus told the Pharisees in John 8:44 that they were of their father the devil who was a murderer from the beginning and he speaks lies. Cain killed his brother and said he did not know where he was. These are the children of Satan (disobedience) from the line of Cain, the seed of the serpent (unrighteousness) that God prophesied about. After admonishing

Cain for his actions, God cast him from his presence and marked him, warning seven years of vengeance on anyone who killed Cain. Upon Cain's exit from the presence of the Lord, he went to a city to the east of Eden called Nod. There are two notes in verse 16 that are important; one is that Eden was a place where the garden was. In fact, *Strong's Concordance* H5731 (Eden) means the region of Adam, his home. Also, the root word (*Strong's Concordance*, H5727; `Eden) means pleasure: delicate or delight. Therefore, the understanding of Adam and his wife leaving the garden would indicate they went home. Home to a place that was a pleasure to be, even if they had to work hard to survive. However, on the other hand, Cain went to Nod, a place that was full of vagrants (*Strong's Concordance*, H5113). In Nod, Cain had a son named Enoch (not the one who walked with God). Enoch had an interesting grandson named Lamech (not Noah's father). Lamech made a declaration that he had killed two men, and if his great-grandfather Cain, who killed one man would be avenged sevenfold, then he, who had killed two, would be avenged seventy and sevenfold. This was a clear display of his pride and self-worth. This statement declared him to be above all else (having no God).

I find it interesting that in Genesis 5:3, 130 years passed before Adam knew his wife again, producing their third son, Seth. Coming to the close of Genesis 4, we find that Adam and his wife continued to trust God. We find this to be true within Eve's statement about her third son with Adam from their second knowing (verse 25). Here, Eve makes a declaration that God had appointed her another seed instead (in place of) of Abel (righteousness). The birth of Seth reinstituted righteousness back into the line of Adam the living soul. This action was initiated by the atonement actions of Abel (giving the blood sacrifice which restored the righteous relationship with God). This is indicated in verse 26 when the declaration of men beginning to call upon the name of the Lord. The importance of this is in Romans 10:13 when Paul writes that "whoever calls upon the name of the Lord shall be saved." Being that the word of God is true, then what applied in Paul's time and what applies in our time applied at the beginning with the descendants of Seth the son of Adam, the son of God (Luke 3:38).

IS THE GOSPEL YOU ARE BEING TAUGHT
THE TRUE GOSPEL OF JESUS CHRIST?

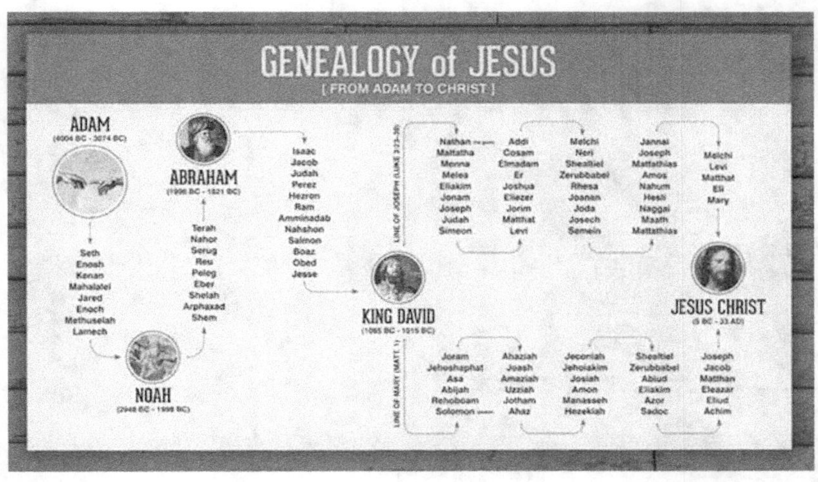

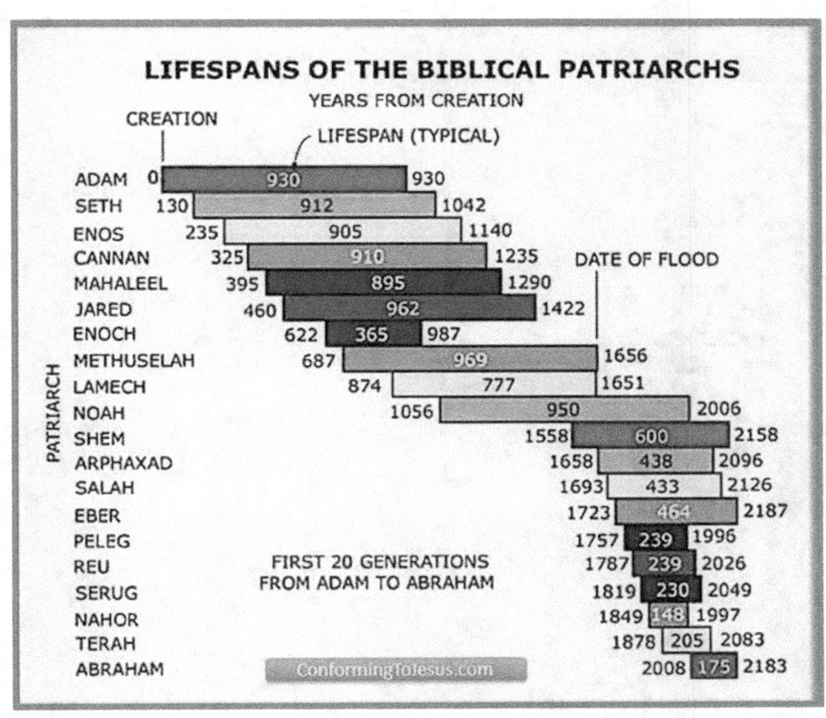

Adam to Noah

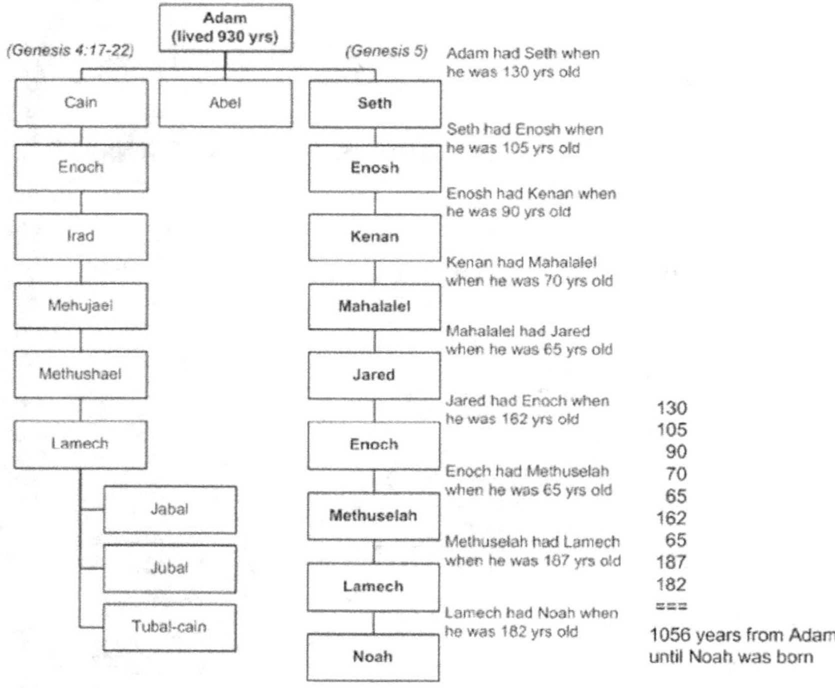
Adam
(lived 930 yrs)
(Genesis 4:17-22)
(Genesis 5)
Cain
Abel
Seth
Enoch
Enosh
Irad
Kenan
Mehujael
Mahalalel
Methushael
Jared
Lamech
Enoch
Jabal
Methuselah
Jubal
Lamech
Tubal-cain
Noah
Adam had Seth when he was 130 yrs old
Seth had Enosh when he was 105 yrs old
Enosh had Kenan when he was 90 yrs old
Kenan had Mahalalel when he was 70 yrs old
Mahalalel had Jared when he was 65 yrs old
Jared had Enoch when he was 162 yrs old
Enoch had Methuselah when he was 65 yrs old
Methuselah had Lamech when he was 187 yrs old
Lamech had Noah when he was 182 yrs old
130
105
90
70
65
162
65
187
182
===
1056 years from Adam until Noah was born

Noah to Abraham

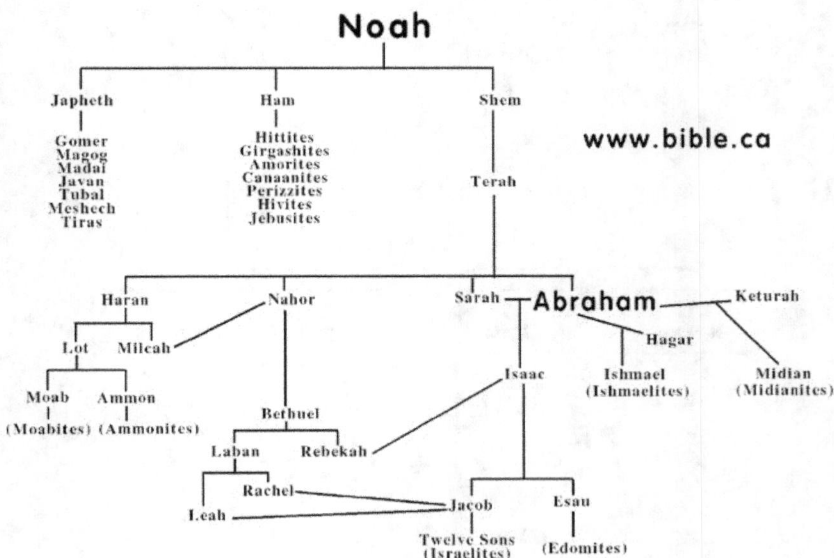

Abraham's Family Tree from Noah

Abraham to Jesus

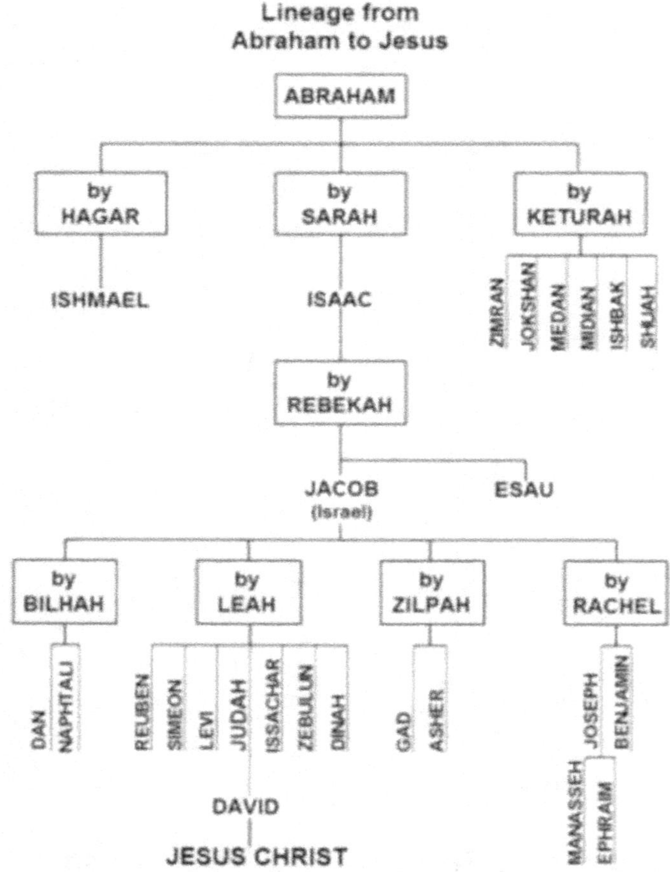

There are some interesting points to be made about the family of Adam. If we look at Genesis 4 and 5, we find the division of the family, one under the house of Cain (the unrighteous) and one under the house of Seth (the righteous) chapter 4. However, in chapter 5, there is no mention of Cain and his descendants until chapter 6. They are known as the daughters of men (Cain) who caught the eye of some of the sons of (Adam). Another important point is Adam died (eight hundred years after Seth's birth or the eighth generation)

at the birth of Methuselah. This means Adam walked and taught his descendants about the natures of God. Note, according to the chart, Noah, Shem, and Abraham live together for a time. This is important in that Abraham possibly received knowledge and understanding about what happened before the flood by two that were there.

Children of the Day and Night

As we venture on in the final area of this narrative, we will find some shocking knowledge; the main aspects of our teachings are lacking. It is not my objective of proving one thing or another. My objective is to determine, why does this matter? As I mentioned above, review your narrative about the nature(s) of man. I started this because, in order to understand your narrative, you must know who you are and whose you are. You see, there are the children of the day (righteous light) and children of the night (unrighteous, darkness) (1 Thess. 5:5). This division started in the beginning with Cain and Abel, not Adam and his wife. Understanding God's word, Paul tells us to "study to show yourself approved unto God, able to rightly divide the word of truth." The shocking aspect of Genesis 5 comes in verses 1–3. In these verses, we find that everything in the Bible from Genesis 5 to Revelation 22 is about the generations of Adam (verse 1), that in the day they were created, they both were named Adam. This is important because when someone says Adam caused this or that, we must understand which Adam was being spoken of or about (1 Tim. 2:14). Here we find that Adam (male) did not go into transgression, but the woman did. Okay, for all of you who are crying about this by saying, "But nothing happened until Adam (male) ate," remember, the two were one, and what impacted one impacted the other. However, the woman only had a position but not status, while Adam had position and status. This means she had nothing to defuse the effects of the evil portion of the fruit from the tree. Because he (Adam) had a link with God via the Spirit of God, the spirit of truth that is God's nature (righteousness), filtered the evil out and made it harmless (Rom. 8:1, 28). This is because, with the Spirit of God (truth) in you, there is no condemnation and all things work for the good. Because of his status with God, this applied to Adam (male) as well, being the living soul from the beginning.

Genesis 5 clears up a lot about the creation of man. The primary narrative teaches us that Adam and his wife produced all the people of the earth after leaving the garden, and doing so, all men were given an evil nature, which needed redemption. This implies that there was no escape or remission from evil until Messiah sacrificed on the cross (Heb. 9:22). As mentioned above, Abel gave an offering of his firstling of the flock, a blood offering, and God accepted it. At the same time, in the spirit, the Lamb of God was being slain (Rev. 18:24) for a sacrifice for the transgressions of the Adams. The last two aspects of this project may have you looking at your narrative into the creation and nature of man as a whole. The first thing we learn is that Adam and his wife lived 130 years outside the garden in the land of Eden before begetting Seth. During this time in Genesis 5, there is no mention of other children, not even Cain or Abel. In fact, verse 3 indicates that after 130 years, Adam begot a son in his own likeness and image. Wait a minute, are we not taught that man is in the likeness and image of God (Gen. 1:26), right? What are you to believe and what does it mean to be in the likeness and image of Adam? If you are confused, maybe rereading this narrative along with your Bible will clear some things up (just saying). Good and evil runs on parallel tracks, running side by side but never crossing. This is what the meaning of Matthew 7:17 is: good trees bear good (righteous) fruit and corrupt trees bear evil (unrighteous) fruit. Note: It is not the fruit that is good or evil, but the seed.

Remember, whatever your narrative is, God's master plan is not governed by it. His plan will conclude at the coming of a new heaven and a new earth and the descending of the new Jerusalem (Rev. 21:1).

WHO IS JESUS?

Jesus, The Heretick

Was Jesus a heretic during his time on earth? To answer this question let's do what we always do, go to the Bible. In the scriptures, the word heresies are mentioned three times (1st Corinthians 11:19, Galatians 5:20, and 2nd Peter 2:1) while the word heretick is mentioned once (Titus 3:10). Both words come from the Greek language and carry the same meaning. Strong concordance G141 indicates that the meaning of the word heretick is, "fitted or able to take or choose a thing," schismatic, factious, a follower of a false doctrine". The dictionary states that heresies are, "opinion or doctrine at variance with the orthodox or accepted doctrine, especially of a church or religious system, the maintaining of such an opinion or doctrine of the Roman Catholic Church, the willful and persistent rejection of any article of faith by a baptized member of the church, any belief or theory that is strongly at variance with established beliefs, customs, etc.". The keyword from the strong concordance definition is schismatic. To be schismatic is to be a person with a schism (to be divisive). Therefore, to be a heretic, a person must stray away from a specific doctrine or belief of a religious order or sect. From a Biblical perspective, it is a person who does not believe that Jesus is the King, to whom the law and the Prophets had proclaimed (Acts 18:5-6). Paul tells Titus this concerning his relationship with those who were under the law of sin and death in Titus 1:9-11, "Holding fast the faithful word as he hath been taught, that he may be able by sound doctrine both to exhort and to convince the gainsayers. For there are many unruly and vain talkers and deceivers, especially they of the circumcision: Whose mouths must be stopped, who subvert whole houses, teaching things which they ought not, for filthy lucre's sake". Paul then goes on to further classify these individuals as being hereticks in Titus 3:9-11 when he tells Titus to, "But avoid foolish questions, and genealogies, and contentions, and strivings about the law; for they are unprofitable and vain. A man that is an heretick after the first and second admonition rejects; Knowing that he that is such is subverted, and sinneth, being condemned of himself". Here, Paul has some hard words for those who are declared to be hereticks. Is this why the Pharisees continued to declare Jesus and the Apostles including Paul as blasphemers. Strong Concordance tells us that a blasphemer (G989) is someone who, "speak evil, slanderous, reproachful, railing, abusive". Was this what the religious leaders were referring to in Matthew 26:64-65 when Jesus stood before the high priest and said, "…Thou hast said: nevertheless I say unto you, Hereafter shall ye see the Son of man sitting on the right hand of power, and coming in the clouds of heaven. Then the high priest rent his clothes, saying, He hath spoken blasphemy; what further need have we of witnesses? behold, now ye have heard his blasphemy". However, Jesus proclaimed who he was to the woman at the well. In John 4:21-26 we find this conversation, "Jesus saith unto her, Woman, believe me, the hour cometh when ye shall neither in this mountain nor yet at Jerusalem, worship the Father. Ye worship ye know not what: we know what we worship: for salvation is of the Jews. But the hour cometh, and now is, when the true worshippers shall worship the Father in spirit and truth: for the Father seeketh such to worship him. God is a Spirit: and they that worship him must worship him in spirit and truth. The woman saith unto him, I know that Messias cometh, which is called Christ: when he has come, he will tell us all things. Jesus saith unto her, I that speak unto thee am he". The action of the woman is a true indication that she knew exactly who Jesus was, the Christ. Now, from a Church's historical perspective, a heretic is a person that does not follow the Apostolic Creeds as laid down by the Roman Catholic Church. These include those protestant groups that follow those creeds as part of the Gospel of Christ. Within the world today, many religions include many gospels of who Jesus is or is not.

But, let us stay in the area of our question, was Jesus a heretic during his time on earth?

From the beginning, there have been two opinions. In 1 Kings 18:21, Elijah asked the people this, "And Elijah came unto all the people, and said, How long halt ye between two opinions? if the Lord be God, follow him: but if Baal, then follows him. And the people answered him not a word". We can even go back further to where Moses asked the people "who was on the Lord's side?". The fact is that there must always be heretics. In 1st Corinthians 11:18-19, Paul tells us this, "For first of all, when ye come together in the church, I hear that there be divisions among you; and I partly believe it. For there must be also heresies among you, that they which are approved may be made manifest among you". We see that heresies are here to separate truth from error. Now to answer the question, Jesus could not have been a heretic because to be a heretic, a person must either disregard, deny, or not know the Law and Prophets declaration about the Kingship of Jesus, the Christ. However, the ruling groups of his time, the Sadducees, and the Pharisees considered him a heretic because he went against what they were teaching the people. They were teaching them they needed to keep the Law of Sin and Death by following them because they knew best and that they would intercede to God for them. In other words, the religious leaders wanted to continue spoon-feeding the people with false teachings. This was completely different from what Jesus was teaching. He taught that he was the Christ, the physical image of the invisible God (Colossians 1:15), the one that the Law and the Prophets indicated. His message to the people is found in Matthews 4:17 which reads, "From that time Jesus began to preach, and to say, Repent: for the kingdom of heaven is at hand". The fact that Jesus taught the disciples this message as he went throughout the cities. Jesus's mission was to preach the Kingdom. This is confirmed in Matthew 24:14, "And this gospel of the kingdom shall be preached in all the world for a witness unto all nations; and then shall the end come". Therefore, it was the ruling leaders and those that followed them that were the heretics. All of this goes back to the new commandment of loving one another which leads to doing the father's business.

You Must Be Born Again

Many protestant Christian movements today based their belief system on one central expression. This expression is "You must be born again". Therefore, what does the expression "being born again" mean. This movement tells us that "being born again" restores a person into a righteous relationship with God with the ability to be a witness for Him. The concept of this movement is centered around the presence of sin and how we must manage it daily. From my research, I have found several movements that are based on this expression are following Saint Augustus's third-century doctrine of the original sin. Also, there is a mixture of John Calvin's sixteenth-century doctrine known as the "TULIP". Within the concept of the "TULIP", the "T" is the primary character because it identifies how Calvin and Augustine viewed the man (Adam) and by extension the whole human race as being "TOTALLY DEPRAVED". Now, being that there is no Hebrew or Greek definition of the word "DEPRAVED" that I can find in the strong concordance, we are left with the dictionary's definition which is, "corrupt, wicked, or perverted". It must be noted here that God never calls Adam (the living soul) corrupt, wicked, or perverted, he only saw him as his Son (Luke 3:33). Along with the Augustine and Calvin doctrines were also the Pelagius and Armininian student's doctrines of having a Free Will to accept or not accept God's rule. Although both of these doctrines are based on the doctrine of the original sin as declared by the council of Nicaea in the 4th century AD, they both have the same starting point which is the "FALL OF MAN". The two primary movements that I found interesting in modern times are the Evangelical movement and the Pentecostal movement, they both in some way or another proclaim these doctrines. It is noticed that within both of these movements, they imply there is no remission of sin and that Christians although being saved from sin by the blood of Christ continue in sin. They continue to proclaim that sin still has some type of existence in a Christian's life. The evangelical movement tells us that we are all sinners (Romans 3:23) and must suffer to endure until the return of Christ.

On the other hand, those of the Pentecostal movement indicate that being born again has two stages, one is the saving stage and the other is the power stage. They indicate that a person can be saved from sin, but until you have been empowered by the power of the Holy Spirit with the evidence of speaking in a Heavenly language, you cannot do battle with the devil and by extension sin. Under the belief of both movements, a person who is washed with the blood of Christ must continue to fight their sinful nature and keep their foot on the devil's neck to control him.

Now, the initiation of the expression "you must be born again" started with those movements which are evangelical by doctrine in the late 1960s. Several other movements around the world hold fast to this doctrine. The focus of these movements is the conversation that Jesus had with Nicodemus in John 3. Let us take a closer look at the expression that has become an integral part of the Christian life. This is the conversation the Nicodemus had with Jesus in John 3:1-7, "There was a man of the Pharisees, named Nicodemus, a ruler of the Jews: The same came to Jesus by night, and said unto him, Rabbi, we know that thou art a teacher come from God: for no man can do these miracles that thou doest, except God be with him. Jesus answered and said unto him, Verily, verily, I say unto thee, Except a man be born again, he cannot see the kingdom of God. Nicodemus saith unto him, How can a man be born when he is old? can he enter the second time into his mother's womb, and be born? Jesus answered, Verily, verily, I say unto thee, Except a man be born of water and the Spirit, he cannot enter into the kingdom of God. That which is born of the flesh is flesh, and that which is born of the Spirit is spirit. Marvel not that I said unto thee, Ye must be born again". We find here that Nicodemus is of the sect of the Pharisees. This sect was responsible for the religious and political wellbeing of the Children of Israel. They walked a thin line between their following the Law and the Prophets and Caesar the Roman God-King. Many who read this conversation, focus on the matter that Nicodemus came to Jesus at night, then conclude that he was sneaking around out of fear. There is no indication of this and this is another conjecture that has been added to the Christian story. Now, we know that Nicodemus not only respected Jesus but also knew who he was according to the Law and the Prophets. This is based on his two opening statements. One was that "no man can do the miracles", indicating the verification of the Law and the Prophets as to the coming of Christ. And the other is, that God was with him, indicating that he identified him as the Christ, who was with God at the beginning (John 1). If we look at what Jesus told Peter in Matthews 16:17, "And Jesus answered and said unto him, Blessed art thou, Simon Barjona: for flesh and blood hath not revealed it unto thee, but my Father which is in heaven". Therefore, the only way Nicodemus could identify Jesus's status and position was that the Father in Heaven reveals it to him. Paul (who was a Pharisee) said this in Galatians 1:15-16, "But when it pleased God, who separated me from my mother's womb, and called me by his grace, To reveal his Son in me, that I might preach him among the heathen; immediately I conferred not with flesh and blood". Therefore, the only way Nicodemus and the other Pharisees he represented could have known this, was by a clear understanding of the Law and the Prophets, as revealed to them by the Father which was in Heaven. As we continue, Jesus's reply to him of being able to see and enter the Kingdom of Heaven was based on two things, water, and the Spirit. Now, if we dive further into this conversation, the essence of being born again is the two things that Jesus indicated as being essential, which were being born of water and the Spirit. I find Jesus's reply interesting because, within the Bible, water is always viewed as a purifier. It is what God used to activate growth in Genesis 2:5, what he cleaned the earth within Genesis 7, and what we use to identify with the death, burial, and resurrection of Jesus. We say that it is an outward expression of an inward act. Now the inward act is the receiving of the Holy Spirit whose job it is to seal us, guide us, and bring us to all truth about the Kingship of Jesus (Ephesians 1:13). The Holy Spirit symbolizes a reality of truth and throws light on both Jesus's nature and mission. It is what always connects us to Jesus our King, Emmanuel. In John 18:37, the conversation between Pilate and Jesus about the truth went like this, "Pilate, therefore, said unto him, Art thou a king then?

Jesus answered Thou sayest that I am a king. To this end was I born, and for this cause came I into the world, that I should bear witness unto the truth. Every one that is of the truth heareth my voice". Now looking at the water and the Spirit in the context of being "born again", it is to be someone who is "of the truth". Another interesting reply of Jesus was that he compared the two natures of man which are the flesh (unrighteousness) and the Spirit (righteousness) as being essential in determining the new birth. In his reply to Nicodemus in John 3:6, he said, "That which is born of the flesh is flesh, and that which is born of the Spirit is spirit". Here Jesus separated the fleshly nature of man from his spiritual nature. The importance of this is that Paul, in Galatians 5:17, says, "For the flesh lusteth against the Spirit, and the Spirit against the flesh: and these are contrary the one to the other: so that ye cannot do the things that ye would". We find here that the flesh and the Spirit are contrary to each other. In strong concordance (G480), contrary means, "to be set over against, opposite to, to oppose, be adverse to, to withstand". The indication in verse 6 by Jesus is that you cannot see nor enter the Kingdom of Heaven if you are born under the nature of the flesh as Paul indicates. Now, from my perspective, Jesus's conversation with Nicodemus was based on what was necessary for a person to see and by extension enter the Kingdom of God. This is what Jesus knew about the sect of the Pharisees as found in Matthews 23:13-15, "But woe unto you, scribes and Pharisees, hypocrites! for ye shut up the kingdom of heaven against men: for ye neither go in yourselves, neither suffer ye them that are entering to go in. Woe unto you, scribes and Pharisees, hypocrites! for ye devour widows' houses, and for a pretense make long prayer: therefore ye shall receive the greater damnation. Woe unto you, scribes and Pharisees, hypocrites! for ye compass sea and land to make one proselyte, and when he is made, ye make him twofold more the child of hell than yourselves". Jesus had some hard words for the sect of the Pharisees. However, I find it interesting that in verse 13, he condemns them for shutting up the Kingdom from men. In other words, they were not teaching about the Kingdom of Heaven but only teaching the concept of making more men that were like them (verse 15) which were children of hell. They were bringing them to the door (Jesus) but then had them go back in the world to make more disciples like themselves. He said that the converts they were making were twofold worse than them. Can these woes that Jesus declared be identified today? In today's Christian culture, the emphasis on sin and Satan is mind-blowing to me. We act as if there is no solution to the sin and Satan situation. Our action toward defeating the forces of evil (the flesh) appears to be nonexistent. Although we have been taught and declare that Jesus defeated sin and Satan at the cross, we also believe he did not complete his assignment (mission) of saving his people from their sins. We do know that Jesus's people (his sheep, his chosen, his elect), were given to him at the foundation of the world (Ephesians 1:4).

As we continue with "You Must be Born Again", the question is what does this look like? To understand this, we must explore the final objective of being born again. That objective is to obtain eternal life in the Kingdom of Heaven with the Lord, the King. Well then, we are taught that our righteous connection with the Lord is our primary concern. Strong concordance G2962 tells us that the Lord refers to Jehovah or Jesus and it means; "belonging to the Lord. Also, G2962 continues its meaning as to, "he to whom a person or thing belongs, about which he has the power of deciding. This title is given to God, the Messiah". Therefore, to be born again is to belong to the Lord to be used by him and for him as he sees fit. So then, what does born again look like? The Prophecy of the Scriptures tells us that the core of being born again and by extension having eternal life is rooted in faith. In Hebrews 11, we are told the value of faith and what is accomplished by it. Looking at verses 1 -3, we find this, "Now faith is the substance of things hoped for, the evidence of things not seen. For by it the elders obtained a good report. Through faith, we understand that the worlds were framed by the word of God so that things that are seen were not made of things that do appear". In verse 3, we see that the worlds were framed by the word of God, Jesus, the image of the invisible God. Do you think this is interesting? Oh well, let us continue. Is it possible that faith is the core of being born again, or is being born again the core of faith? The important question is,

"Which comes first, faith or being born again"? Now, based on what Jesus said to Nicodemus, that being born again is the act of being regenerated by the water and the Spirit, the logical answer would be, that faith in the regeneration of the washing and the newing of the Spirit (Titus 3:5) is the starting point of becoming born again with the final destination being accepted into the Kingdom of Heaven. Now, this acceptance into the Kingdom happens at the moment of the new birth (Matthews 4:17) and is accompanied by the establishment of eternal life in Christ. Next, we find that faith is the core of the new birth, is something that cannot be seen and it is a partner with hope. Hope, in the strong concordance (G1680), Hope is, "in the Christian sense joyful and confident expectation of eternal salvation…". We find here that faith is the foundation of hope, and hope is what reminds us that we as born -again believers are well and that Jesus is with us, Hebrews 12:5. The confirmation of this is found in Romans 8:15 where we are told that the Spirit that we received gives us the ability to cry out "Abba Father". Paul tells us in 1st Corinthians 3:10-11, who the foundation is. He goes on to say, "According to the grace of God which is given unto me, as a wise master builder, I have laid the foundation, and another buildeth thereon. But let every man take heed how he buildeth thereupon. For other foundation can no man lay than that is laid, which is Jesus Christ". Our understanding then is that faith is knowing who Jesus is. Knowing that he is the King, gives the born-again Christian their platform to boldly witness to the world that Jesus is the King and God of heaven and Earth. Acts 4:13 states, "Now when they saw the boldness of Peter and John and perceived that they were unlearned and ignorant men, they marveled; and they took knowledge of them, that they had been with Jesus". The complete understanding of this is found in strong concordance G4102 where it states that faith is the "conviction of the truth of anything, belief; in the New Testament, it is the conviction or belief respecting man's relationship to God and divine things, generally with the included idea of trust and holy fervor born of faith and joined with it. Relating to God, the conviction that God exists and is the creator and ruler of all things, the provider and bestower of eternal salvation through

Christ. Relating to Christ, a strong and welcome conviction or belief that Jesus is the Messiah, through whom we obtain eternal salvation in the kingdom of God". What does the word Christ mean? We have been taught that Christ is the last name of Jesus, Jesus Christ. However, in strong concordance G5548, Christ means, "to anoint and consecrate Jesus to the Messianic office, and furnishing him with the necessary powers for its administration that endure Christians with the gifts of the Holy Spirit". One of the attributes of being born again is receiving the gifts of the Holy Spirit. Paul outlines these gifts in Galatians 5:22-23 which are, "But the fruit of the Spirit is love, joy, peace, longsuffering, gentleness, goodness, faith, Meekness, temperance: against such there is no law". He further reaffirms this in Ephesians 5:9. We find here that Paul does not indicate many of the things that have been injected into what the fruit (gift) of the Holy Spirit truly is. We find here that Christ is the Messianic office of the anointed and consecrated physical image of the invisible God, God in the flesh. Now, this office has been around from the beginning and is the position of the person that conducts God's business and is in a righteous relationship with God. Therefore, it is faith in the fact that we are born again to have life in Christ and be hidden in God (Colossians 3:3). As born-again believers, we have a good report with God (Hebrews 11:2). This report is not based on what we do or don't do, it is based on who we are in the eyes of God (his children). The final note here is that we as bornagain believers are not running from sin and Satan but accepting our place in eternal life in heavenly places with Christ. Now, Paul reminds us of this in Romans 6:1-7, "What shall we say then? Shall we continue in sin, that grace may abound? God forbid. How shall we, that are dead to sin, live any longer therein? Know ye not, that so many of us as were baptized into Jesus Christ were baptized into his death? Therefore we are buried with him by baptism into death: like as Christ was raised from the dead by the glory of the Father, even so, we also should walk in the newness of life. For if we have been planted together in the likeness of his death, we shall be also in the likeness of his resurrection: Knowing this, that our old man is crucified with him, that the body of sin might be destroyed, that henceforth we should not serve sin. For he that is dead is freed from sin". Also, as born -again believers, we are justified, glorified, and sanctified by the Holy Spirit (Romans 8:30 and 15:16). Therefore, we as born-again believers are sealed by God to be who he wants us to be to do his works of spreading the fact that Jesus is Lord, King, and Emmanual after the order of Melchisedec. Many of our leaders today overlook what is said in Hebrews 6:1-3 from the Message Bible, "So come on, let's leave the preschool fingerpainting exercises on Christ and get on with the grand work of art. Grow up in Christ. The basic foundational truths are in place: turning your back on "salvation by self -help" and turning in trust toward God; baptismal instructions; laying on of hands; the resurrection of the dead; eternal judgment. With God helping us, we'll stay true to all of that. But there's so much more. Let's get on with it"!

Knowing that "being born again" is very important in the life of Christians, there must be some more to it. As we explore the Scriptures concerning this, we find that John, the one that initiated this expression assists us in coming to a better understanding of it. In 1st John 5, we see John's in -depth explanation about being born again without using the expression. Here, he indicates that believers' love for Jesus Christ and the one who begotten and sent him to us is the glue that makes being born again works. He goes on to tie our love for Christ and the Father to our love for one another. This is the final new commandment that Jesus left us with (John 13:34 - 35). John goes on to tell us that this new commandment is what gives believers victory over the world. Now, here is an interesting thing, In verse 6, he says, "This is he that came by water and blood, even Jesus Christ; not by water only, but by water and blood. And it is the Spirit that beareth witness because the Spirit is truth". Now, many are taught that this identifies what happen at the cross when Jesus was pierced in the side and water and blood came out. However, John indicates that the water and blood were the way Jesus came into the world in a spiritual and natural sense. To continue, This verse is intriguing to me because it identifies the two essentials of being born again as indicated in John 3. John now gives us the perspectives of those essential and adds another one to it, the blood. We now know that Jesus came by water and blood and the Spirit verified it as being true. This is further confirmed in 1st Timothy 3:16 when Paul tells us this, "And without controversy great is the mystery of godliness: God was manifest in the flesh, justified in the Spirit, seen of angels, preached unto the Gentiles, believed on in the world, received up into glory". Here we find that God was manifest in the flesh (water and blood) and justified (verified) by the Spirit. This is the whole creation story from the beginning to the ascension all wrapped in a mystery. What do you think? So, if we look at the added essential, we find that the blood symbolizes life (Genesis 9:4). This is because the blood is the life force of the flesh. However, the blood that was in the flesh of Jesus served another purpose. We find in Hebrews 12:24 this, "And to Jesus the mediator of the new covenant, and to the blood of sprinkling, that speaketh better things than that of Abel". Now, this brings with it a question of how Abel's and Jesus's blood relate? Looking back at Genesis 4 and the bringing of the offerings, we have been taught that Cain was sent from God's presence because his offering was not his best. However, if we look at verses 10 -12 after the murder of Abel, God tells Cain this, "And he said, What hast thou done? the voice of thy brother's blood crieth unto me from the ground. And now art thou cursed from the earth, which hath opened her mouth to receive thy brother's blood from thy hand; When thou tillest the ground, it shall not henceforth yield unto thee her strength; a fugitive and a vagabond shalt thou be in the earth". The understanding here is that Abel's blood was crying out for justice against Cain. An interesting thing about this comes from Matthews 23:33 -36 after Jesus had pronounced the Woes on the Pharisees and the Scribes. He tells them why they have been judged and found guilty. Here is what he said to them, "Ye serpents, ye generation of vipers, how can ye escape the damnation of hell? Wherefore, behold, I send unto you prophets, and wise men, and scribes: and some of them ye shall kill and crucify; and some of them shall ye scourge in your synagogues, and persecute them from city to city. That upon you may come all the righteous blood shed upon the earth, from the blood of righteous Abel unto the blood of Zacharias son of

Barachias, whom ye slew between the temple and the altar. Verily I say unto you, All these things shall come upon this generation". We find here that blood is very important to God because it speaks to him. Jesus in Matthews 26:28 said his blood was for the remission of sins. That remission of sins was for the Pharisees and those that followed them. The relationship between Abel's and Jesus's blood is that Abel's blood cried out for justice from the ground and Jesus's blood cried out for mercy from the cross. This relationship between these two individuals' blood is remarkable. As I understand it, this situation placed God in a place of judgment. There needed to be a decision as to which were to be honored, justice (punishment) or mercy (forgiveness) on the Pharisees and those that followed them for what they and their forefather the devil had done to God's children. At the cross, Jesus asked for mercy when he said this in Luke 23:43, "Then said Jesus, Father, forgive them; for they know not what they do. And they parted his raiment, and cast lots". As an answer to this request, we find that the veil was torn by God from top to bottom when Jesus cried out this in Matthews 27:50 -53, "Jesus when he had cried again with a loud voice, yielded up the ghost. And, behold, the veil of the temple was rent in twain from the top to the bottom; and the earth did quake, and the rocks rent; And the graves were opened, and many bodies of the saints which slept arose, And came out of the graves after his resurrection, and went into the holy city, and appeared unto many". As a result, God removed the Jewish Sanhedrin completely from their positions of rulership over the Jews. Also, in 70 AD, the temple was destroyed by the Romans and to date, a Muslim Mosque sits in its place. Jesus's prophecy came true.

As we continue with the essentials of being born again, with the combination of the three essentials, we understand that it is the water that purified Jesus for his arrival, it was the blood that identified his speaking life force, and the Spirit influencing believers of the truth, Jesus is the longawaited Christ. Now, after the verification of who Jesus is by the Spirit (the King), we notice that there is a record in heaven, and this record is supported and certified. Before we continue, let us look at the word "record" from the strong concordance. In the concordance, the word "record" (G3140) means, "to be a witness, to bear witness, an example of this is to affirm that one has seen or heard or experienced something, or that he knows it because he has been taught by divine revelation or inspiration". The keyword here for "record" is "witness". In verse 7, we see that this record (witness) is made by the Godhead. The verse reads as follows, " For there are three that bear record in heaven, the Father, the Word, and the Holy Ghost: and these three are one". Now, this record is supported by the three that were there in the beginning. The Father, which strong concordance (G3962) identifies as, "God is called the Father of the stars, the heavenly luminaries, because he is their creator, upholder, ruler of all rational and intelligent beings, whether angels or men, because he is their creator, preserver, guardian, and protector". The Word, which strong concordance (G3056) identifies as, "In John, denotes the essential Word of God, Jesus Christ, the personal wisdom and power in union with God, his minister in creation and government of the universe, the cause of all the world's life both physical and ethical, which for the procurement of man's salvation put on human nature in the person of Jesus the Messiah, the second person in the Godhead, and shone forth conspicuously from His words and deeds". And the Holy Ghost, which strong concordance (G4151) identifies as, "the spiritual nature of Christ, higher than the highest angels and equal to God, the divine nature of Christ". Now, this is what is referred to as the Godhead (Colossians 3:8 -12). We know that this Godhead has existed from the beginning. We find that in Hebrews 13:8, Jesus is the same yesterday, today, and forever. Eternity: Past, Present, and Future as outlined in Revelation 1:7 -8, "…I am Alpha and Omega, the beginning and the ending, saith the Lord, which is, and which was, and which is to come, the Almighty". With Jesus being who he says he is in these verses, then he has always been the image of the invisible God, the container of the Godhead. Colossians 1:15 tells us that Jesus is, "Who is the image of the invisible God, the firstborn of every creature". As we look further into being born again, an interesting thing appears, Genesis 2:1 indicates that Heaven and Earth were finished at the same time, with everything occupying its position as the hosts of God. Therefore, Heaven and Earth together are partners in God's master plan. Jesus told the apostles this in Matthews 16:19, "And I will give unto thee the keys of the kingdom of heaven: and whatsoever thou shalt bind on earth shall be bound in heaven: and whatsoever thou shalt loose on earth shall be loosed in heaven". They were given the keys to Heaven and the authority to control what goes on in Heaven and Earth as keepers of the promise of eternal life. As mentioned, heaven and earth have to exist as one to bring about the complete plan of God which is both doing his bidding as he sees fit. Therefore, in verse 8 of 1st John 5, we find that there is also a combined witness within the earth. It says, "And there are three that bear witness in earth, the Spirit, and the water, and the blood: and these three agree in one". The interesting thing about this is that the word "witness" has the same meaning as the word "record". This is what ties heaven and earth together which is the Spirit, the water, and the blood. In Genesis 1:2, we understand that the face of the deep and the earth was in darkness and the Spirit of God moved upon the face of the waters. Next, God spoke and light came into existence. John tells us in John 1:4 that in the Word was life and that life was the light of men. Is it possible that the first thing that God spoke into existence was his image? Just saying. Could this be the living soul that God blew his Spirit into at the beginning? Within the schools of thought, there is an understanding that Genesis 2 come before Genesis 1 because nothing activated on earth until after it rained and the man was formed Genesis 2:5. Study to show yourself approved. Now, why is this important, you see the same Godhead that supported and certified the record as to who Jesus is, the King in heaven, is the same Godhead that supported and certified the witness as to who Jesus is, the King in the earth. This is because they (the Godhead) are one and they agree as one. That agreement on earth is that Christ is the image of the invisible God, the firstborn of all creatures, Colossians 1:15. What then does this have to do with being born again, well just as Christ had to be supported and certified to be the King, each of us must be supported and certified to see and enter the Kingdom. That support and certification in heaven and on earth happened at the moment we understand that Jesus is the Christ from the beginning and that he is always with us here on earth.

Jesus's Ascendants

In order to understand who Jesus is, we must follow his earthly lineage. The common teaching today is that Jesus is the son of David, the long-awaited Messiah. Based on Matthew, his bloodline runs from Abraham to Mary. On the other hand, Luke declares his bloodline runs from Adam to (supposedly) Joseph. The difference between these two lineages is the division at the heirs of David. We find in Matthew the lineage leads from David to Solomon (the fifth son from Bathsheba) and leads to Mary. However, the lineage in Luke leads from David to Nathan (the fourth son of Bathsheba) She was given the right to name him by David and Nathan. It is believed to be in honor of Nathan the Prophet. This action led to Joseph, who is the (supposed) father of Jesus. The importance of this must come in another series. For now, let us focus on "who is Jesus?"

The Jesus's Story: His Mission

One of the most controversial individuals in the universe has proven to be this person named Jesus, who was born to take the position of the Christ (the Messiah after the order of Melchizedek, the King over all creation) and have the status of the Priest of the Most High God (mediator between God and man). Born over two thousand years ago, he is still atop the list of people who are both loved and hated at the same time. Well then, when did the controversy about him become all that is said and written about? Some say at the time of his adult ministry (thirty years after his birth), others say at his birth (at the transition of the Old Testament to the New Testament), while it is also said at the beginning of time, when the living soul was formed from the ground. The question then is which (if any) of these hypotheses are right? In addition, there is a teaching that Jesus is the incarnation of God (God in the flesh). Many declare that this happened at his birth. However, is this the true answer? To answer this question, we much first define his (Jesus) mission to humanity, then his purpose to the world, and finally his position in eternity. So then, let us explore the first aspect of what was or is Jesus's mission to humankind.

It is indicated that he came to save his people from their sins (Matt. 1:21). Many have taken this and other verses to finalize Jesus's mission. However, it is noted that being the Savior is only a part of who he is and what he had to do. Notice here, he is defined as the Savior of his people and not the world. It must be understood that there are two worlds: one where Satan supposedly is the influencer and another where Jesus is God. The evidence of this comes from the statement made in Matthew 12:32, "And whosoever speaketh a word against the Son of man, it shall be forgiven him: but whosoever speaketh against the Holy Ghost, it shall not be forgiven him, neither in this world, neither in the *world to come*" (emphasis mine). Dangerous stuff. Now, let us look back at the question of "what was his people's sins?" The word "sin" in *Strong's Concordance* G264 means "to be without a share in; to miss the mark; to err, be mistaken; to miss, or wander from the path of uprightness and honour; to do or go wrong; to wander from the law of God, violate God's law, sin." I would like to focus on the phrase "to wander from the law of God." We find in Malachi that God imposed curses on the priests for misrepresenting him to the people and having them violate God's laws about their dealing with him. Could this be the sins that Jesus needed to save his (those given him by God, John 17) from? Come to your conclusion.

In order for us to understand his mission, we must find out whose he is and where he came from. The answer to this question lays in the garden. As mentioned before, in the beginning, a prophecy was given in Genesis 3:15, "And I will put enmity between thee and the woman, and between thy seed and her seed; it shall bruise thy head, and thou shalt bruise his heel." So now we find that war is pronounced by God between the woman and the serpent (Gen. 3:13–16), with the combatants being the seed of the woman and the seed of the serpent. Who is the seed of the woman and the seed of the serpent? Paul tells us in Galatians 3:16 that "Now, to Abraham and his *seed* were the promises made. He saith not, as to *seeds*, as of many; but as of one, and to thy *seed*, which is Christ" (emphasis mine). So we find here that the seed singular is Christ who we call Jesus. There is a belief that the singular indication here is the seed of the woman (believe it or not). On the other hand, John tells us in 1 John 3:8–13,

> He that committeth sin is of the devil; for the devil sinneth from the beginning. For this purpose, the Son of God was manifested, that he might destroy the works of the devil. Whosoever is born of God doth not commit sin; for his seed remaineth in him: and he cannot sin, because he is born of God. In this, the children of God are manifest, and the children of the devil: whosoever doeth not righteousness is not of God, neither he that loveth not his brother. For this is the message that ye heard from the beginning, that we should love one another. *Not as Cain, who was of that wicked one,* and slew his brother. In addition, wherefore slew he Able? Because his own works were evil, and his brothers were righteous. Marvel not, my brethren, if the world hates you. (Emphasis mine)

The highlighted phrase here is on the twelfth verse, which indicates that Cain was of the wicked one. Cain was the manifestation of the unrighteous seed of the wicked one, when the woman ingested the seeds from the tree of good and evil, while Abel was the manifestation of the righteous seed. It must be noted that Adam (male) has never been identified as being the wicked one; however, he remained the Son of God (Luke 3:38). Can I digress? God talks a lot about seeds. An interesting thing came to my remembrance. In Genesis 1:28, man is told to be fruitful. Now, fruit is the byproduct of seed, right! Why didn't God say be seedful? Could it be that God provides the seed (good or evil) to each individual as he sees fit? Anyway, this is a sidebar. Let us continue. This is also mentioned above, in the fact that Adam was not punished for listening to his wife. In fact, the punishment was placed on the ground. Also, in Genesis 3:22, Adam was given god status because he knew good and evil and was able to discern between the two and choose the good. To understand this, let us explore Hebrews 5:14, "But strong meat belongeth to them that are of full age, even those who by reason of use have their senses exercised to discern both good and evil." An Old Testament scripture to compare with this is Deuteronomy 30:19, "I call heaven and earth to record this day against you, that I have set before you life and death, blessing and cursing: therefore choose life, that both thou and thy seed may live." We find here that life and death, blessing and cursing refer to good and evil. God's command is to "choose life (blessings and good)." In addition, there are no options but to do within God's commands.

Now, going back to the garden, the serpent told the woman that God knew when their eyes were open they would know good and evil. Is this a good or bad thing? It must also be noted that Adam is in the direct bloodline of (sinless) Jesus; only the devil ("And the great dragon that was cast out, that old *serpent*, called the devil, and Satan, which deceiveth the whole world: he was cast out into the earth, and his angels were cast out with him" [Rev. 12:9]) can claim the title of the wicked one. In Zachariah 5:5–8, we find him talking to the Lord of host about the contents of a basket. When Zechariah looked in the basket, he saw a woman in it. The Lord of host explained the following: "Then the angel who talked with me came forward and said to me, 'Lift your eyes and see what this is that is going out.' And I said, 'What is it?' He said, 'This is the basket that is going out.' And he said, 'This is their iniquity in all the land.' And behold, the leaden cover was lifted, and there was a woman sitting in the basket! And he said, 'This is Wickedness.' And he thrust her back into the basket, and thrust down the leaden weight on its opening" (ESV). Now, I is of the male gender. However, if what Zechariah saw in the basket is true (and it is), then Satan, who is the wicked one, the embodiment of wickedness, is a chameleon that has masqueraded as someone she is not. Her offspring possesses this same characteristic. This passage of scripture shines a light on 2nd Corinthians 11:15. The *Strong'* *Concordance* gives us several meanings to the word "wickedness." The one relating to Zechariah 5 is H7564, which is the feminine noun, which means "guilt, wickedness in civil relations, of enemies, ethical and religious." This word, as a verb (action), H7561 means "to condemn as guilty in civil relations, in ethical or religious relations, and to act wickedly in ethics and religion." In Isaiah 34, he talks about a time when God was very angry with the nations. It was a time of wholesale desecration and desolation. My interest here is in the area of verse 14. There he talks about a creature called a "screech owl". The creature is important because Isaiah identifies it as; "… The night-demon Lilith, evil, and rapacious, will establish permanent quarters (MSG). The Strong Concordance H3917 defines it as, "Lilith," name of a female goddess known as a night demon who haunts the desolate places of Edom". In the dictionary, it is, "Lilith", a Semitic Mythology. "a female demon dwelling in deserted places and attacking children. Jewish Folklore. Adam's first wife, before Eve, was created". Be approved unto God, do your Bible research. Anyway, let's move on.

Now that we have some indication as to who the seed of the woman and the seed of the serpent is, we can conclude that 1 John 3:8 is talking about Jesus. Therefore, his primary mission was to (past tense) destroy the works of the Cain, the seed of Satan.

Now to end this part, his mission began in the beginning at the prophecy to the woman and ended at the cross.

> Though he were a Son, yet learned he obedience by the things which he suffered; And being made perfect, he became the author of eternal salvation unto all them that obey him; Called of God a high priest after the order of Melchisedec. (Heb. 5:8–10)

Now, this is a very interesting occurrence. Jesus is a High Priest after the order of Melchisedec. This is a person who many say is a kind of Christ. No one can be like Christ, because there is only one Christ (Jesus). How then can Jesus be of his priestly order if he is lesser than Jesus on all levels? In order to understand this, we must understand what a priestly order is and who can grant it. The granting of something to or on someone means there is a direct link (contact) between the granter and the grantee. There is no in-between person. Therefore, in order for Melchisedec to have a priestly order means it was God that granted it to him. This made him the caretaker of the order. Now, if we say Melchisedec's priesthood was granted to him by God and this happened in the beginning, within the order of Melchisedec, there are two titles. You see, Melchisedec was the king of Salem and the priest of the Most High God (Hebrews 7:1–3). In the history of humanity, there have been only three that held both titles at the same time: Adam, Melchisedec, and Jesus. Jesus is the last to ever hold them (1 Corinthians 15:45–49). This would mean that Adam, Melchisedec, and Jesus are one and the same person, for they all are called the Son of God (Heb. 7:3, Luke 3:38, and John 10:36). This is a sidebar, let us continue.

Therefore, it can be safely said that his mission is finished. John 19:30 indicated the completion of the mission: "When Jesus therefore had received the vinegar, he said, *It is finished*: and he bowed his head, and gave up the ghost" (emphasis mine). What was finished? The power of the works of the devil over the children of God. Romans 5:14 tells us that there is a group of people who were not under the sin of the transgressor Adam (the woman). A further indication of this is found in 1 Kings 19:18, where God tells Elijah that he has seven thousand that had not bowed to Baal and had not kissed him. Paul writes in Romans 11:4, "But what saith the answer of God unto him? I have reserved to myself *seven thousand* men, who have not bowed the knee to the image of Baal" (emphasis mine). Jesus saved his people (the children of God) from the sin of wander from the path of uprightness and honour (*Strong's Concordance* G264) by following unrighteous leaders (Malachi 1 and 2). They are the ones Jesus talks about in John 17. They are also the ones that Jesus covers from the grip of sin. Romans 8:9 states, "But *ye are not* in the flesh, but in the Spirit, if so be that the Spirit of God dwells in you. Now if any man has *not* the Spirit of Christ, he is none of his" (emphasis mine). Finally, this was accomplished when he assumed his position as Lord of lords. Revelation 17:14 tells us that "these shall make war with the Lamb, and the Lamb shall overcome them: for he is Lord of lords, and King of kings: and they that are with him are called, and chosen, and faithful."

Jesus's Story: His Purpose

Now, after looking into the mission of Jesus, let us take a look into his purpose in the world. In Matthew 1:23, we are told that when he was born, he would be called Emmanuel, which the Scriptures interpret as "God with us." The question is, When was there a time in history (His-story) that God was not physically with us? If God did not physically interact with his people before the birth of Jesus, then who did Abraham talked within Genesis 17:1–3? Who was that who said to him, "And when Abram was ninety years old and nine, the Lord appeared to Abram, and said unto him, 'I am the Almighty God; walk before me, and be thou perfect. And I will make my covenant between me and thee, and will multiply thee exceedingly.' And Abram fell on his face: and God talked with him…"? Was this not Abram's Jehovah God? Anyway, just my perspective. From this position, we find that Jesus assumed all authority to execute judgment (John 5:27). We find in Hebrews 2:6 the statement of "What is man?" It must be noted that this question is not talking about man as in plural but man as in the singular. *Strong's Concordance* H120 declares man (`adam) in the plural sense as a masculine noun, while H121 declares man (`Adam) in the singular sense as a proper masculine noun. In the verse mentioned above, the writer here is referring to man (Adam, H121) in the proper noun perspective. The identity of this person is revealed in verse 9 where it states, "But we see Jesus." If we are to believe and understand Hebrews 13:8, Jesus has always been the physical image of God, God in the flesh. Not at his birth but at the beginning when God formed him from the ground outside of the garden and blew the breath of life in him. Genesis 2:19 tells us that when God formed everything he had formed in the garden, he brought them unto Adam (*Strong's Concordance*, H121). Adam, who is the living soul filled with the Spirit of God, called the name of all God had created. Ephesians 3:8 tells us that Jesus the Christ created all things. In John 1:3, the Word of God made all things and nothing could be made without him (The Word of God speaks as God). If this is true (and it is), then Jesus is the form from the ground that God blew his breath in and became a living soul.

Defining the purpose of Jesus is to understand who he is. For you see, Jesus's purpose was the only message he ever preached: "the Kingdom of Heaven is at hand" (Matt. 4:17). This meant that at his appearance, the manifestation of God's kingdom on earth was completed and accessible to all those he called. Those that had been given to him (John 17:12, 20). Jesus tells us in John 10:27–30 that his sheep hear his voice and follow. He also continues to say that the Father gave them to him and no man is able to pluck them out of his Father's hand. This is because he and the Father are one and the same. You must understand what Paul meant in Romans 5:14 when he wrote about the reign of death over them that sinned after the similitude of Adam's transgression; how Adam is the figure of him that was to come (Jesus).

It must be noted here that this is the main verse used to indicate that Adam sinned. However, if we look closer, we see that the writer is referring to the transgression of Adam. In 1 Timothy 2:14 we learn that Adam was not deceived, but the woman was deceived and went into transgression. In addition, Genesis 5:2 states that God called their name Adam in the day they were created. Again, in Genesis 2:23 Adam declared that they were one because she came out of him. This is how she got her first name Wo-man, man out of man (Adam out of Adam).

As we close this narrative, the questions are still out there. Is the doctrine you are being taught the true Gospel of Christ our God or not, and why does it matter? In John 5:39 Jesus tells the Jews that they search the Scriptures in search of eternal life; however, to get eternal life, they needed to come unto him. We are taught that coming to Jesus means we must be able to recite this or that scripture or say this or that prayer. Many say to know him is to sacrifice for him. While others teach, believe it, and receive it in Mathew 6:33, "But seek ye first the kingdom of God, and his righteousness; and all these things shall be added unto you." In First Corinthians 1:30, we are told, "But of him are ye in Christ Jesus, who of God is made unto us wisdom, and righteousness, and sanctification, and redemption." We find here that Jesus is the righteousness of God. We are further told in Hebrew 11:6, "But without faith, it is impossible to please him: for he that cometh to God must believe that he is and that he is a rewarder of them that diligently seek him." Our reward comes when we diligently seek him (Jesus). This is done when he calls you unto him to be used when, and how he wills. An important note here is the faith we live by is his faith and not ours. Paul tells us in Romans 1:17, "For therein is the righteousness of God revealed from faith to faith: as it is written, the just shall live by faith." He is quoting from Habakkuk 2:4, where it is said, "Behold, his soul which is lifted up is not upright in him: but the just shall live by his faith." It is God's faith that reveals his son to them that are called. Jesus outlines in John 3:16 that "whosoever believe." Have you ever thought about what is it we must believe about Jesus? Could it be that he can heal you, bring you prosperity, or fix the things you think needs fixing? The Scripture indicates that we must believe in him in order to get eternal life. However, the common teaching is that we must believe "on him" in order to receive this or that. Did you know that believing "on him" is working from the outside, trying to get in? This is why present-day teaching is always about God getting ready to do this or that. We are told, just a little while longer, just hold on. On the other hand, to "believe in him" is to trust from the inside, knowing that God has completed all things. Philippians 1:6 says, "Being confident of this very thing, that he which hath begun a good work in you will perform it until the day of Jesus Christ."

Why does this matter? If you are confident in him in the fact that he is the living soul, then you will understand that because you are his, he will never leave you nor forsake you. Why? Because you are dead, and your life is hidden with Christ in God (Col. 2:3). All things work for the good. Therefore, Jesus's purpose in the world is to bring order to chaos. He did this by being the caretaker (King) of God's kingdom on earth and the priest of the Most High God, the mediator between man and God. He has succeeded in his purpose by being the great influencer of God's nature. This is why he could say in Matthew 4:17, "From that time Jesus began to preach, and to say,

Repent: for the *kingdom of heaven* is at hand."

Jesus's Story: His Position and Location

The last aspect of this narrative will be, "What position is Jesus within eternity?" In Hebrews 5:9 we find that in his obedience, he was made perfect and became the author of our eternal salvation. Now, "salvation," is imparted unto those who obey him. John 3:16 tells us that our salvation is based on our belief in him. Our belief that he is God's Son, the King, and Messiah of Earth. We are taught that he is at the right hand of the power of God (Matt. 26:64). It is important here to listen to what Jesus says in John 20:16–22. He said, "Jesus saith unto her, Mary. She turned herself, and saith unto him, Rabboni; which is to say, Master. Jesus saith unto her, Touch me not; for I am not yet ascended to my Father: but go to my brethren, and say unto them, I ascend unto my Father, and your Father; and to my God, and your God. Mary Magdalene came and told the disciples that she had seen the Lord, and that he had spoken these things unto her. Then the same day at evening, being the first day of the week, when the doors were shut where the disciples were assembled for fear of the Jews, came Jesus and stood in the midst, and saith unto them, Peace be unto you. And when he had so said, he shewed unto them his hands and his side. Then were the disciples glad, when they saw the Lord. Then said Jesus to them again, Peace be unto you: as my Father hath sent me, even so send I you. And when he had said this, he breathed on them, and saith unto them, Receive ye the Holy Ghost." Why was it important for Jesus to ascend to the Father before they could touch him? In John 17:5, we are told this by Jesus, "And now, O Father, glorify thou me with thine own self with the glory which I had with thee before the world was." He went to the Father to reclaim his glory. *Strong's Concordance* G1391 states glory is "a thing belonging to God, a thing belonging to Christ. The kingly majesty of the Messiah."

Now, these accounts about Jesus indicate that he is in heaven, at the right hand of power, and preparing a mansion for us. I find this interesting but not complete. We know he went to heaven, we know he is at the right hand of power (Acts 7:56), and we know he is preparing a place for us. My interest here is that we have been taught that we are going to heaven. However, in 1 Thessalonians 4, we are told that we will meet him in the air and forever be with him. Here in 1 Thessalonians and Revelation 19:11, Jesus is coming to make war on the unrighteous, not going back to heaven. It must be noted that those with him are the called, chosen, and faithful. Is this His children (1 Peter 2:9, Ephesians 1:4, and Luke 16:10)? As to him being at the right hand of power; could that be in the new Jerusalem where the mansions are? If so, the new Jerusalem will be coming down from heaven to earth in order to finalize the establishment of his kingdom on earth. Can it be that the kingdom is the place where the temple of God is and where God stays and abides? In this first instance, Jerusalem, in the Old Testament, was the place that the Jews believed that God's Spirit resided, in the ark, in the temple, where the people worshipped (John 4:19), a place built by hands. However, in the New Testament, the saints are taught that the body is the temple of the Holy Spirit (1 Cor. 6:19–20). This is where the Spirit of God dwells. Therefore, the house of God is his believers, for his seed remains in us because we are born of God.

The Inheritance of the Saints

Let us continue. Hebrews 1 indicates to us that the Son was appointed heir to all and he made the worlds. It further states that his word is power, that he purged sins and is set down on high. Verse 4 of Hebrews 1 identifies him as being better than angels with a more excellent inherited name. There is a declaration by God that he never called an angel "Son." Now then, God said that all the angels were to worship him (his Son).

WHAT'S ON YOUR MIND?

Throughout the New Testament, we are taught about the different aspects of the mind and how it is important to understand it. Romans 1:28 talks about a "reprobate mind" which is given by God. We find in 1 Corinthians that we are to be perfectly joined in the "same mind." While in Colossians 3:12, the "humbleness of mind" is an attribute of the elect of God. The most classic case of this is Romans 7, where Paul talks about the struggles between sin that is within the law. His indication is that the law is good, but sin has corrupted it. It is corrupted when people's focus is on the pleasures of the body. He reminds us in verse 4 that we (believers) are dead to sin, because of what Christ did, that his death frees us from the bondage of sin and all its trappings. However, being free from sin in our members does not mean the mind is also. When the mind is trapped, its understanding is cloudy. The cloudiness comes from the war between the law of the bodily members (the law of sin and death) and the law of within the mind (the law of life in Christ). The former enforces keeping the letter of the law of sin and death, declaring it is the only way to please God. While the latter strengthens our understanding that the law of life has set us free and that we have already pleased the Father by loving his Son. Present-day teaching informs us to repent (turn from) and confess (ask for forgiveness) of our sins. After looking into this teaching further, I found that "repent" in the *Strong's Concordance* G3340 means "to change one's mind [i.e. to repent, to change one's mind for better], heartily to amend with abhorrence [hatred] of one's past sins." We find the root word G3539, which means "to perceive with the mind, to understand, to have understanding, to think upon, heed, ponder, consider." In other words, to repent is to think about something differently with understanding.

Repentance is to have a new perspective of something but not taking action on it. God did this in Exodus 32:14, where it is said, "And the Lord repented of the evil which he thought to do unto his people." Once again, we are taught to repent and confess, but in Acts 3:19, we are told to "repent ye therefore, and be converted, that your sins may be blotted out when the times of refreshing shall come from the presence of the Lord." So does repentance leads to confession or conversion? Now we see here that it is the conversion that leads to acceptance by God. *Strong's Concordance* G1994 is "to turn, to the worship of the true God, to cause to return, to bring back, to the love and obedience of God, to the love for the children, to love wisdom and righteousness intransitively, to turn to one's self, to turn one's self about, turn back, to return, turn back, come back." We can see that the action word here is to be converted. The question is, Who does the converting, us or God? Ephesians 1:4 says, "According as he hath chosen us in him before the foundation of the world, that we should be holy and without blame before him in love." What is your answer? Now there are many other scriptures indicate that our mindset is very essential in our dealings with God.

Now, seeing that the mind is an essential part of our being a blessed believer or not, let's look at what is the meaning of the mind. *Strong's Concordance* G5426 states that the word *mind*, in conjunction with Philippians 2:5, indicate that it is to have the understanding and to be wise. Therefore, to have the mind of Christ means to have godly understanding and wisdom. However, there is a dictionary sub-meaning of it which states, "to have an opinion of one's self, think of one's self, to be modest, not let one's opinion (though just) of himself exceed the bounds of modesty." So to have the mind of Christ is to have confidence in (me, myself, and I) as being led by God, but keeping that understanding in proper perspective. This is why Paul could talk about his confidence in God, who began a good work in us, would keep us (Phil. 1:6).

It must be understood that before we begin our believer's journey, our minds must have been transformed. There are two scriptures in the New Testament that talk about the transforming of the mind, one negative and one positive. This is a good indication of the comparison between good and evil. In 2 Corinthians 11:14–15, we are told that Satan and his ministers have been transformed into an angel of light and ministers of righteousness. It also tells us that their works will determent their end. Paul sums it up in Philippians 3:17–19:

> Brethren, be followers together of me and mark them which walk so as ye have us for an example. (For many walks, of whom I have told you often, and now tell you even weeping, that they are the enemies of the cross of Christ: Whose end is destruction, whose God is their belly, and whose glory is in their shame, who mind earthly things.)

You see, because they only focus on things and stuff and not bringing believers into the full understanding of who they are, and whose they are, then their end is set for destruction. Their primary thing is to play with people's minds. However, in Romans 12:2, we are told not to conform to this world, by having our minds transformed into the will of God. Now we see these two mind transformations, one toward Satan and the other toward God (Jesus). Therefore, a question presents itself: who does the transforming of the mind and for what purpose? Many say that we (man) can transform our minds. We are told, if you just get more word (Bible) in you, then your mind will be transformed, and then stay away from wickedness. Others say that the Holy Spirit does it, but it is a process that takes time and you must show evidence. However, Titus 3:5 dictates that the mercy of God regenerates and renews us by the Holy Spirit. Now, the most interesting thing about this is that the verse states it is not by righteous works. Titus also tells us that Jesus has covered us with his Spirit on us abundantly in order that we are justified and are made heirs to eternal life. Therefore, we find that it is God, by his Spirit, that transforms our minds either for good or evil. Why is this so? Because it is a part of his master plan of transforming this earth (which was void and without form) into his kingdom. Also, there is no indication that our mind transformation happens over a period of time. Because God, who is outside of time, does his work always in the present, and when he says it, then it is done. Paul explains in Galatians 5, "But when it pleased God, who separated me from my mother's womb, and called me by his grace, to reveal his Son in me, that I might preach him among the heathen; immediately I conferred not with flesh and blood." The only important thing in our life is not what God has done in the past nor what he is going to do in the future, but what he is doing in the present. Our God is a right-now God.

There are several aspects of the mind as outlined in *Strong's Concordance*; however, they all identify the mind as being the center of understanding (G1097). Proverbs 4:7 comes to mind because it states, "Wisdom is the principal thing; therefore, get wisdom: and with all thy getting get *understanding*." Therefore, the link between Christ and his followers is their mindset. It must be noted that the word *let* only comes with two options: to do or not to do. Rather what a person does or doesn't do is based on who they are and whose they are. For not to do is a sin: "But be ye doers of the word, and not hearers only, deceiving your own selves" (Jas. 1:22). John confirms this in 1 John 3:9 when he states, "Whosoever is born of God doth not commit sin; for his *seed* remaineth in him: and he cannot sin, because he is born of God" (emphasis mine). There is a saying, "The mind is a terrible thing to waste"; or more commonly put, "The mind is a terrible thing."

Man's Behavior: Psychology

In the world of science, the practice of understanding the mind falls under the category of psychology. Psychology is the science of the mind or its mental states of processes. It deals primarily with the behavior of humans. Some people believe that it can profile (identify) an individual based on their mental behavior. Therefore, it has become the art of being able to control a person by influencing their mental inputs. It has been long known that psychology and religion have common aspects. Psychology and religion are comparable because they both operate in the environment of the human psychic. This is important because a person or entity (spirits) with the right psychic inputs can control the behavior of others. There are many incidents in the Scriptures that indicate people and entities influenced a group or someone. Now, 1 King 22:22 is a clear example of how a group was influenced by an entity: "Now, therefore, behold, the Lord hath put a *lying spirit* in the mouth of all these thy prophets, and the Lord hath spoken evil concerning thee" (emphasis mine). There is a warning in 2 Corinthians 11:3 that says, "But I fear, lest by any means, as the serpent beguiled Eve through his *subtilty*, so your minds should be corrupted from the simplicity that is in Christ" (emphasis mine). An important note about psychology is that there are two elements of it: one focuses on the needs of individuals while the other focuses on the needs of the group. We find that needs are those things we feel are required, necessary, or obligated to have in order to ensure our well-being. In the *Strong's Concordance*, "need" is associated with G5306, to be behind, to suffer want, or to be devoid of. On the other hand, G5532 is associated with necessity, duty, or business. Any way we look at it, needs are tools that can be used for good or evil. Paul tells us in Philippians 4 that God shall supply all our needs. Needs are important in that they are a key attribute that determines how we adjust to our environment and others.

Now, within the world of psychology, there are two basic theories concerning the understanding of human behavior: one is Douglas McGregor's management behavioral theory of theory X and theory Y and the other is Abraham Maslow's theory of the hierarchy of needs. Many leaders, both secular and religious, who deal with influencing individuals operate within some aspect of psychology. Because in their position as people influencers, they have a need to be able to profile (understand) individuals in order to keep some kind of order within the group. The problem comes when their influence becomes addictive to the people. This is confirmed in Malachi when God cursed the priest (religious leaders) for misleading the people. Jesus himself scolded the money changers of defiling the house of prayer in Matthew 21:13 because they were teaching the people that it was okay to buy deformed and unclean animals to sacrifice.

Let's not be alarm about the control and power the influencers may have over a group (good or evil). God has designed this into his master plan. If we take a closer look at this mind thing, we will see that it runs along the same track as good and evil. Understanding that within the precept of having the mind of Christ, there must be the concept of having the mind of the Antichrist. 1st John 4:3 tell us that spirit of antichrist will come and is already in the world. If there is a good, then there must be evil, to balance things out. The confirmation of this is in Revelations 22:14–15, which says, "How blessed are those who wash their robes! The Tree of Life is theirs for good, and they'll walk through the gates to the City. But *outside* for good, are the filthy curs: sorcerers, fornicators, murderers, idolaters—all who love and live lies" (emphasis mine). So you see, evil will be always present, even after the new heaven and new earth comes. The difference is that now, we are spiritually separated from sin and it has no more dominion over us because we are dead to it. However, in the end, we will be physically separated from sin and all its components—for good.

Primary Theories of Behavior

Now, let's take a look at the two basic behavioral theories that govern human behavior. Douglas McGregor's theory of controlling human behavior focuses on the governing concept of how managers control their workers in order to complete a task.

Douglas McGregor's Theory X and Y

Within his concept of theory X, he says that some managers deal with their workers from a mindset that "people dislike work, have little ambition, and are unwilling to take responsibility and need constant supervision." When you think about it, this is the way that many leaders, both secular and religious, see some of those they work with. A good example of this that some leaders (secular and religious) spent a lot of time telling the people they need to do a little bit more to get this or that. There is a constant teaching of failure or not measuring up to some standard. So within theory X, the leader determines what each member of the group needs in order the get them to complete the task. On the other hand, theory Y "highlights the self-motivating role of job satisfaction and encourages workers to approach tasks without direct supervision." These are the managers that rely basically on the creative abilities of their worker and see them in the light as a coworker. Granted, there are those in this group that may need close supervision, however, the managers allow the other workers to assist in this matter. Now, the successful task completion rate does not indicate which management style is best. It only indicates the types of motivational factors that can be used to get the task done by the group. Asking ourselves, how do these theories play into religion? Theory X lends its techniques more in the direction of the legalist religious leaders. Because they primarily make people feel that the only way to God was to go by them. Their basic concept is, "Bring it to me and I will give it to God." Their belief was man-given status and position. My understanding is that this was the way of the children of Cain (darkness). What did Jesus say to the religious leaders of his day?

> Ye are of *your father the devil*, and the lusts
> of your father ye will do? He was a murderer
> from the beginning, and abode not in the truth,
> because there is no truth in him. When he spea-
> keth a lie, he speaketh of his own: for he is a liar,
> and the father of it. (John 8:44; emphasis mine)

However, these theories do not lend themself to any of the teachings of Jesus. He taught the precept of teaching God's ways to others so that they could go out and teach them to others. Jesus's method of teaching developed leaders, not followers. All of Jesus's disciples later became apostles (followers to leaders). In doing so, he reminded his people who they were and where they came from. This precept enabled them to become all God wanted and needed them to be. The parable of the sower and seed is a good indication as to what God wants from us. He wants us to come to the understanding of who and whose we are and spread the kingdom. In Matthew 13, this parable is explained: "Then Jesus sent the multitude away, and went into the house: and his disciples came unto him, saying, Declare unto us the parable of the tares of the field. He answered and said unto them, He that soweth the good seed is the Son of man; The field is the world; the good seed are the children of the kingdom; but the tares are the children of the wicked one." Note: We are taught that the good seed is the Word (the Bible), but Jesus said it is the Children of the Kingdom (God); us. Is Jesus right or wrong?

McGregor's chart

McGregor's Theory X and Theory Y		
Theory X	**sphere**	**Theory Y**
Dislike work, find it boring, will avoid if we can	ATTITUDE	Need to work, want to take an interest, we can enjoy it
Must be forced or coerced into compliance	DIRECTION	Direct ourselves towards an accepted target
Need to be directed, avoid responsibility	RESPONSIBILITY	Thrive on responsibility
Motivated by fear, lack of money, lack of job security	MOTIVATION	Motivated by the desire of self-development and to contribute to the world
Little creativity, except when getting around rules	CREATIVITY	Highly creative when given recognition and opportunity

Unlike McGregor, who showed how an individual could use the tools of his theories in order to influence the needs of a group to get a task completed, Maslow worked more on how each individual operates within the basic needs of survival. Using the concept of a pyramid, he separated the basic needs into two classes: physical and psychological.

Abraham Maslow's Hierarchy of Needs

Within the class of Maslow's physical needs are those things that a person cannot do without. They consist of level 1: air, water, food, sleep, group stability, body fluid releasing, and reproduction (sex). These all are basic internal physical needs. The lack of any of these needs (for a period of time) will result in death. The second level of physical needs class is considered to be external basic needs. These needs are primarily based on the actions or inactions of others. They are security (safety), work, obtaining supplies, have a sense of group morality, ownership, and health. These two levels of the class of physical needs are the primary ones that many influencers focus on. As we move on to the next class of needs, we find they are psychological. These levels are very important in that they involve external mental inputs. The third level and the first class of psychological needs is love and belongingness. This class of psychological needs is based on one's relationship with others. This one is the give-and-take actions of one toward another. Within the love and belongingness class of needs, there is friendship, intimacy, trust, and acceptance. It comprises of the feeling of being a part of the group. It must be noted that this is the primary level of needs that many Christians hang out at. We are constantly being taught that our belonging to a group is what gives us fulfillment. The feeling of true happiness is being in a group of like-minded people to call on in times of need. The teaching that the good of the group is more important than the good of the one is commonly accepted. A common worldly expression is that "the good of the many outweighs the good of the one" (*Star Trek*). However, Luke 15:4 tells us, "What man of you, having a hundred sheep, if he loses one of them, doth not leave the ninety and nine in the wilderness, and go after that which is lost until he finds it?" You see, in the eyes of the Lord, the good of the one outweighs the good of the many. The value of this is, the one knows that when they go off into the unknown that the shepherd will come and get them. Paul tells us in Hebrews 13:5 that in any situation we find ourselves in, the Lord will never leave us nor forsake us.

Now, coming to this understanding, an individual is ready to move to the next level of needs, which is self-esteem. Within the operations of self-esteem, we find the need for one to feel good about themselves. The class of need consists of esteem of oneself, dignity, achievement, mastery, and independence. The value of this class is that it gives the individual the ability to operate inside or outside of the group. They realize that their success or failure is determined by the Lord as they obey him. At this point, the individual begins to scrape away the need of following and/or belonging to a group or person. Their relationships now are based more on mutual agreements with others than by reacting to a feeling of being lonely or excluded.

The last level on the pyramid within psychology is the class known as self-actualization. Self-actualization is the level of individual needs that bring a person to the conscious mindset of realizing their personal potential, with a strong knowledge of self-fulfillment, and a high level of being self-motivated to become all that God needs and want them to be. It must be noted that at this level, one is preceded as being prideful and conceited. However, Paul indicates that this is a mindset of confidence (Phil. 1:6). Within the world of self-actualization, the individual sees things as they are and not how they want them to be. If we take a closer look at self-actualization, we find that this is the objective of every believer: to operate in their full potential as children of God. Also, within the consciousness of self-actualization is the understanding of who you are and whose you are—a child of God. Galatians 4:9 tells us, "But now, after that, ye have known God, or rather are known of God, how to turn ye again to the weak and beggarly elements, whereunto ye desire again to be in bondage?" Another teaching of Paul within Galatians comes from chapter 4:5–7, where he teaches "To redeem them that were under the law, that we might receive the adoption of sons. And because ye are sons, God hath sent forth the Spirit of his Son into your hearts, crying, Abba, Father. Wherefore thou art no more a servant, but a son; and if a son, then an heir of God through Christ." Self-actualization, in a believer mindset, leads them to the understanding that not only they understand who God is, but more importantly, they realize that

God knows them personally, and he will never leave them nor forsake them (Heb. 13:5).

Maslow's pyramid

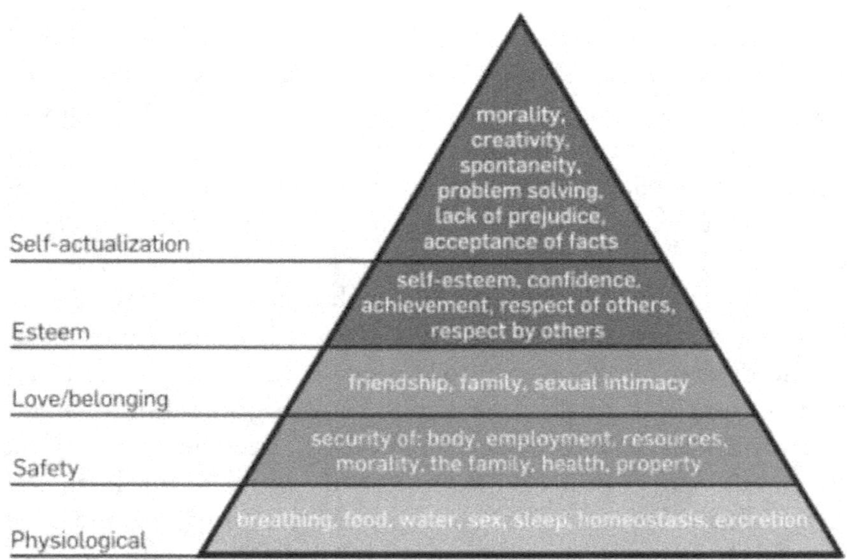

Let This Mind

The question continues on, "Why does it matter?" Well, it matters because there is a connection between what the secular and religious world are attempting; they are attempting to control the minds of those who follow them. They continuously input mindsets that all answers about life come through them or someone like them. In order to understand this or that, all you need to do is read this or that book and go to this or that conference. However, Hebrews 8:10 indicates that the Lord does the putting: "For this is the covenant that I will make with the house of Israel after those days, saith the Lord; *I will put* my laws into their mind, and write them in their hearts: and I will be to them a God, and they shall be to me a people" (emphasis mine). It must be noted that he does not say someone else will complete this task. As in the times past, he spoke to the fathers by the prophets, but in these days he speaks to us by his Son. Notice that he is the Word (John 1:1). *Strong's Concordance* has two meanings for the word *word*. One is G3056, which is the logo or written word, and the other is G4487, which is the rhema or spoken word by a living voice. The teaching of the Lord is not to memorize the Bible, as we are taught to do. We are told by the Lord to meditate on these things (2 Tim. 4:15). The things we are to meditate on are conversation, charity, in spirit, in faith, and in purity. John 21:25 informs us, "And there are also many other things which Jesus did, the which, if they should be written every one, I suppose that even the world itself could not contain the books that should be written. Amen." This clears up what is said in Romans 8:26–27 about the job of the Spirit. It says, "Likewise the Spirit also helpeth our infirmities: for we know not what we should pray for as we ought: but the Spirit itself maketh intercession for us with groanings which cannot be uttered. And he that searcheth the hearts knoweth what is the mind of the Spirit, because he maketh intercession for the saints according to the will of God." Here, we see that the Holy Spirit speaks to God for us and returns to us with the answer from God. A question here is, Is the Holy Spirit a living voice that speaks to us? Interesting, you think! Let us continue. Meditate in the *Strong's Concordance* is G3191, which is to care for, attend to carefully, and practice. Therefore, when we are told to meditate on the book of the law (the Bible), it is meant for us to practice what he tells us to do.

> Don't fool yourself into thinking that you are a listener when you are anything but, letting the Word go in one ear and out the other. Act on what you hear! Those who hear and don't act are like those who glance in the mirror, walk away, and two minutes later have no idea who they are or what they look like. But whoever catches a glimpse of the revealed counsel of God—the free life!—even out of the corner of his eye, and sticks with it is no distracted scatterbrain but a man or

woman of action. That person will find delight
and affirmation in the action. (Jas. 1:22–25)

All of these things have to do with the mind and how it can be influenced. Things like the serpent influencing the woman, with a thought about the tree, and Cain being influenced by the thought to rebel against God, and to kill his brother or the sons of God is influenced by the fairness of the daughters of men (another story) and making God angry by rebellion. All this matters because within God's relationship with the man, he looks at the thoughts of the heart. Why does this matter? Well, is the Gospel you are being taught the Gospel of Christ or another Gospel? Galatians 1:6–9 from the Message reads,

> I can't believe your fickleness—how easily you have turned traitor to him who called you by the grace of Christ by embracing a variant message! It is not a minor variation, you know; it is completely other, an alien message, a no-message, a lie about God. Those who are provoking this agitation among you are turning the Message of Christ on its head. Let me be blunt: If one of us—even if an angel from heaven!—were to preach something other than what we preached originally, let him be cursed. I said it once; I'll say it again: If anyone, regardless of reputation or credentials, preaches something other than what you received originally, let him be cursed.

The Gospel or a Gospel

Why does this matter? Well, if you are following the wrong narrative about the nature of man, then you may be following another Gospel. Let us consider, how does one believe in another Gospel? Many who believe in another Gospel are ones who do not understand the concept of the Gospel of God. In Romans 10, Paul tells us about how Israel had a zeal for God but not the righteousness of God. Their zeal was based on an incorrect knowledge of God. How, then, was this possible? If we read verse 4, we find that they did not believe that Christ was the end of the law for righteousness. Paul goes on to explain that the Law of Moses demanded that all who follow it had to keep it without fail. He indicated that the Jews were taught that their salvation was wrapped up inside of the law of sin and death, and there was no way around it. In James 2, he makes a declaration about faith without works. In his statement, he indicates that "For whosoever shall keep the whole law, and yet offend in one point, he is guilty of all." There are many who stand on the foundation of the Mosaic Law as the route to salvation. They profess the strict adherence to the Law is what pleases God and causes him to cover us with his grace that saves us from the evil one. This concept is based on the understanding that we must do this to be redeemed for our false works, rejections, and unbelief, and not measuring up. The concept which is mentioned before relates to maintaining the letter of the Law and not the spirit. "But now we are delivered from *the law*, that being dead wherein we were held; that we should serve in newness of spirit, and not in the oldness *of the letter*" (Rom. 7:6; emphasis mine). Now, what does all this mean? Well, it means that many of our leaders are teaching (knowingly or unknowingly) another gospel, one based on the continual works and the blind obedience to man's philosophy that are full of conjectures and omissions. As mentioned above in Malachi, God cursed the priests for misinforming the people about the will of God. Look at what God told Job's three friends in Job 42:7–9:

> And it was so, that after the Lord had spoken
> these words unto Job, the Lord said to Eliphaz the
> Temanite, My wrath is kindled against thee, and
> against thy two friends: for ye have not spoken of
> me the thing that is right, as my servant Job hath.
> Therefore take unto you now seven bullocks and
> seven rams, and go to my servant Job, and offer
> up for yourselves a burnt offering; My servant

> Job shall pray for you: for him will I accept: lest I deal with you after your folly, in that ye have not spoken of me the thing which is right, like my servant Job. So Eliphaz the Temanite and Bildad the Shuhite and Zophar the Naamathite went and did according as the Lord commanded them: the Lord also accepted Job.

Here the acceptance of Job is based on his testimony that he had not done anything wrong before God. This was the very attitude Job showed to Elihu that made him very angry. This is what Elihu said concerning Job from The Message Bible in Job 35:1–3, "Elihu lit into Job again: 'Does this kind of thing make any sense? First, you say, "I'm perfectly innocent before God." And then you say, "It doesn't make a bit of difference whether I've sinned or not."'" Job's statement appears to be right on target. You see, as children of God, we lean not on our understanding but confess what he tells us because we are in a safe place with him (Col. 3:3). This is an example of what the Gospel will do for you; drive them crazy.

God's Leadership

Why does this matter? Well, God only deals with those leaders he establishes and not those established by men. This concept is the cornerstone of God's leadership team. God's leadership techniques are to develop leaders in accordance with the school of John the Baptist, which taught repent for the kingdom of heaven is at hand. This is the same message Jesus taught in Matthew 4:17. Therefore, our leaders are not preaching the kingdom of heaven (God), and how it affects us. Their teachings are more about getting in the kingdom than being in it. The Scripture states in John 14:6 that no man can come unto the Father but by Jesus; however, in John 6:63–66, Jesus tells the disciples this:

> It is the spirit that quickened; the flesh profited nothing: the words that I speak unto

you, they are spirit, and they are life. But there
are some of you that believe not. For Jesus knew
from the beginning who they were that believed
not, and who should betray him. And he said,
Therefore I say unto you, that no man can come
unto me, except it was given unto him of my
Father. From that time many of his disciples went
back and walked no more with him.

And here 1 John 2:19 states, "*They* went out from *us*, but *they* were not of *us*; for if *they* had been of *us*, *they* would no doubt have continued with *us*: but *they* went out, that *they* might be made manifest that *they* were not all of *us*" (emphasis mine). The manifestation here is delivering an incomplete message about what Jesus taught. They left in contempt about the true message. These were the ones that did not hear his voice and could not follow him.

The Kingdom

The gospel of the kingdom informs those in the kingdom of their responsibility to the King, which is to be his ambassadors. Ambassadors in the concordance are "among the Jews, members of the great council or Sanhedrin [because in early times the rulers of the people, judges, etc., were selected from elderly men], of those who in separate cities managed public affairs and administered justice. Among the Christians, those who presided over the assemblies [or churches]. The NT uses the term bishop, elders, and presbyters interchangeably." Paul tells us in 2 Corinthians 5:20, "Now then we are ambassadors for Christ, as though God did beseech you by us: we pray you in Christ's stead, be ye reconciled to God." It is clear that all children of God are the managers (reconcilers) of his program of reconciliation and is responsible only to him as the King. The importance of this is that within the kingdom of God, there is sovereignty, royalty (deity) power, and dominion. Question, Is there sin in the kingdom? Just asking. Residents in the kingdom are in completely contrast those of the world, which are in bondage, weakness, and have surrendered. You see, those attributes of the world which are the works of the flesh. "Now the works of the flesh are manifest, which are these; Adultery, fornication, uncleanness, lasciviousness, Idolatry, witchcraft, hatred, variance, emulations, wrath, strife, seditions, heresies, Envyings, murders, drunkenness, revellings, and such like: of the which I tell you before, as I have also told you in time past, that they which do such things shall not inherit the kingdom of God" (Gal. 5:19–21). What child of God can claim these attributes? The Lord tells us in 2 Corinthians 5 that we have a ministry of reconciliation. We are to reconcile those who have called upon the names of the Lord (Gen. 4:26). Those who do not remember who they are and whose they are, are just like the son in Luke 15:17 as he realized when he came unto himself how his father's servants had bread to spare while he perishes. God wants us to bring to remembrance those who were in the kingdom and got lost. We are not to do this with words of condemnation but actions of reconciliation. We reconcile those who are his is by our actions and not by persuasion. Actions that are of the fruit of the Spirit. "But the fruit of the Spirit is love, joy, peace, longsuffering, gentleness, goodness, faith, Meekness, temperance: against such there is no law. And they that are Christ's have crucified the flesh with the affections and lusts. If we live in the Spirit, let us also walk in the Spirit" (Gal. 5:22–25). What child of the devil can claim these attributes? The only ones that can come into the kingdom are those who are his that got misdirected and searching for a way back. For as mentioned above, Jesus said, "My sheep knows my voice and will not follow a stranger." If you are not being taught this, then we are being taught another Gospel.

The teaching of the Gospel is the teaching of leadership. In order to teach leadership, there must be an understanding of individuality. God uses individuals who are not in bondage to others or themselves. The reason for this is that only individuals can be given a divine assignment. If we check the Scriptures, God used individuals to conduct his business, and they were only responsible to God. Jesus's church, during his walk on the earth, had only twelve members, all of which he taught as individuals with individual assignments. This is verified in John 21:20–22: "Then Peter, turning about, seeth the disciple whom Jesus loved following; which also leaned on his breast at supper, and said, Lord, which is he that betrayeth thee? Peter seeing him saith to Jesus, Lord, and what shall this man do? Jesus saith unto him, If I will that he tarry till I come, what is that to thee? follow thou me."

What then was it that Jesus taught his disciples? Well, when we look at the relationship between Jesus and his disciples, we find he taught them lessons like the last will be first, blessed are the poor, those given him none has been lost, etc. Before I continue, I found the word "poor" interesting. This is because we are taught that it means those who physically lack something. However, when Jesus referred to the poor, he may have been talking about their spiritual need. *Strong's Concordance* G4430 indicates that "as respects their spirit, destitute of the wealth of learning and intellectual culture which the schools afford [men of this class most readily give themselves up to Christ's teaching and proved themselves fitted to lay hold of the heavenly treasure]." Just saying. But the most powerful thing from my perspective is, that Jesus taught them was that he is the way, the truth, and the life. Why, then, is this important? If we look at the words *the way*—which means action, direction, approach, system, vehicle, etc.—in the context of what Jesus is relating is that he is the only direction to the kingdom of heaven. The fact he is the "truth" dictates that he is the reality all are looking for and that he is the life we are all attempting to become. The totality of this statement is that Jesus is the only direction that we need to come to the reality of understanding our life as to who we are in the eyes of God.

THE COVENANTS

What Is a Covenant?

The first mention of the term *covenant* appears in Genesis 6:18. God is talking to Noah just before the flood. He states he will establish his covenant with Noah and his (Noah's) family. *Strong's Concordance* H1285 identifies a covenant as being an alliance or a pledge between men or God and man. It continues to note that it is a divine ordinance with signs and pledges. The root word of H1254 means to shape, fashion, or create with God as the subject. There are several other phrases associated with this root word. Therefore, a covenant is an agreement that is made by one individual to another, the obligation to keep the covenant rest on the one making the covenant. In the scriptures, it is always God making a covenant with those he selects about how they fit into his plan of humanity. Now, the recipient of the covenant is not under obligation to uphold that covenant unless they make a similar covenant. The reason God makes covenants with his select is because of the relationship they have between each other. A covenant is what binds God and the man together. There is a difference between a covenant, law, and a prophecy. A covenant establishes a guarantee intent while a law gives directions, and a prophecy is a projection of events. There are many covenants God had made with his own. There are only five I will be looking at: the Adamic, the Noahic, the Abrahamic, the Davidic, and the New Covenant.

The First Covenant: Adamic

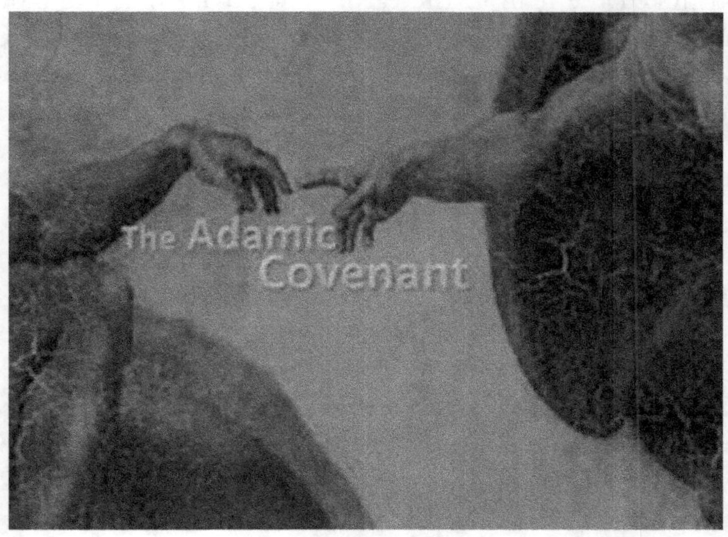

The first guarantee-intended agreement (covenant) God made to the man was when he blew the breath of life into him and he became a living soul. This established the first guaranteed link between God and man. It confirmed that they were one and the same. With God taking this action, he established that he would never leave or forsake the man. Therefore, this was God's first covenant with the man, that he would be his divine representative on earth to rule over it. This covenant is known as the Adamic covenant. This covenant begins with the breath of life in Genesis 2:7; it was enhanced at the proclamation of the man becoming as one of us in Genesis 3:22 and transitioned at Genesis 6:18 when Noah was selected to move forward after the flood. The Adamic covenant was initiated, established, and enforced by God. Adam's establishment of his covenant to God was initiated approximately 150 years after he left the garden when Seth's descendants began to call upon the name of the Lord. This indicated the purging of the family of man—Cain's family nature (unrighteousness) and Seth's family nature (righteousness). Within the Adamic covenant, the main teaching is that it is comprised of three elements: First, the element of linkage by the forming of man from the ground. This action linked the man to the earth. The second was the blowing of the breath of life into the form. This linked the man to God. Finally, the prophecy of the coming seed. This placed a time line on the devil's activities. As mentioned in other parts of the narrative, Adam was linked to God by the breath of life being in him. This covenant was with Adam that he was God's representative on earth. Now there was a prophecy placed on the woman based on her transgressions of looking into the tree of good and evil, and eating thereof. The prophecy of her seed conquering the seed of the serpent in the end. Now as for the sin of Adam, the scripture's first mention of the word sin is to Cain by God in Genesis 4:7 when he indicated that he (sin) was lying at the door waiting to be controlled or to control him (Cain). He described him as someone waiting to claim something. The *Strong's Concordance* H2398 defines sin as "to sin, miss the goal or path of right and duty, to incur guilt, incur penalty by sin, forfeit." The interesting thing here is that sin does not only cause the missing of the goal or path, but it also brings guilt which leads to condemnation for which there is a punishment. To continue, we understand by the actions of Cain that he must have been the seed of the serpent God had mentioned before; the seed of the serpent which was its offspring that would try to interfere with the seed of the woman; the seed that is of the wicked one—Satan. Therefore, sin is only associated with the children of darkness. Sin is like a virus that can only infect those who are not protected. The Adamic covenant only applies to those who carry the seed of the God in them (1 John 3:9). Therefore, all covenants are based on the promise of God given in the garden to the woman about the victory. The essence of the Adamic covenant is for the seed of the woman to be fruitful, multiply, replenish, subdue, and have dominion over it. It must be noted here that we are talking about Adam's chosen offspring that carried the seed of God as mentioned in 1 John 3.

The Second Covenant: Noahic

Although the Noahic covenant is identified in Genesis 6, its initiation is in Genesis 5:29 when Noah was declared as the one to comfort the people concerning their work and toil because of the Lord's curse on the ground (Gen. 3:17). The Noahic covenant consisted of the original Adamic covenant of being fruitful, multiplying, replenishing, subduing, and having dominion. This covenant is one that continues the Adamic covenant while at the same time introduces a new one on the other side of the flood.

Genesis 6 begins with the multiplying of men on the earth. These were the children of Cain and the children of Seth. Now, there is a great difference between these two people. One is the nature of the unrighteous seeds of Cain, the son of serpent, who is Satan (Gen. 4:17), and the other is the nature of the righteous seeds of

Seth, the son of Adam, who is as God (Gen. 4:26). We know in verse 4 that there began a transformation of the spirit of man when sons of God (the line of Seth) and the daughters of men (the line of Cain) came together and wickedness became great. There is a teaching on this subject that dictates that the sons of God were the fallen angels. Again, in Hebrews 1:5 God asks the question about which angel he had called a "My Son." The answer is none. It must be noted that this all happened in the ninth generation of Adam. At this time Methuselah was in his nine hundredth year of life. Methuselah's name means "man of the dart" (*Strong's Concordance,* H4968, with the root word H7971, meaning "a missile of attack"). It is said that at the death of Methuselah, the flood came and destroyed all life that possessed the breath of life. However, the Lord God found grace in Noah and established him as the carrier of the seed (Gen. 6:17), the seed that carried the promise of the final Son of God which would destroy the works of the devil.

Now, God refines the Noahic covenant to a new level. Note: God, who is the King (1 Sam. 8:7), and like a King, cannot erase an edict but can only draw up a new one to replace the old one. God's edict or covenant under the Adamic covenant stated to be fruitful, multiply, replenish, subdue, and have dominion. Also, every herb-bearing seed and tree was to be their meat. In Genesis 9, God blessed Noah and his sons and continues the Adamic covenant, but enhanced some things. Now we see that in God's covenant with Noah, he states that all creatures would fear and dread him (because of his position and status as God representative), and God would deliver them into his hand so he could have dominion. Also, at this time the life force of all creatures and man was rooted in the blood. Within this covenant, God planted a restriction. The restriction was the forbidding of the eating of blood nor the shedding of man blood. For the penalty of such action was the forfeiture of their life force (the blood). The basis of the latter restriction was that man is in the image of God (a representative figure). The conclusion of the Adamic covenant is found in Genesis 9:15 with the final decree to Noah that Noah would be a perpetual generation.

The Third Covenant: The Abrahamic

The Noahic covenant held true until Genesis 14 when Melchizedek appeared and blessed Abraham in verse 19. It must be noted here that Abraham did not just fall out of the sky. His bloodline goes all the way back to Adam through Noah. It is recorded in the book of Jasher that Noah, Shem, and Abraham lived together for thirty-nine years.

Further, it is noted that Noah lived fifty-eight years of Abraham's life, and Shem lived thirty-five years after Abraham died. It is also believed that Shem was Melchizedek that met Abraham on the king's dale. Additionally, there were nine relatives in the bloodline of Jesus that was from Noah to Abraham (Luke 3). This is important because those individuals were carriers of the promised seed. The covenant God made with Abraham can be divided into several parts. In Genesis 15:18 through 17:9, God first made a territory covenant by mapping out the complete location of God's kingdom. God then made a population covenant by ensuring Abraham would multiply exceedingly. Next, God placed him over many nations as their father. Afterward, God established that Abraham and seed (Christ) would have an everlasting covenant with him. And finally, the Abrahamic covenant was a command from God to Abraham that he and his seed would keep the everlasting covenant. Note: this is a command and not a request.

The Fourth Covenant: The Davidic Covenant

The story of the Davidic covenant is one that is activity. It is a continuation of the Abrahamic covenant about the land and God's relationship with Israel. This covenant starts out with the children of Israel being full of unbelief and self-righteousness. In 1 Samuel, we find the elders of Israel came to Samuel and demanded a king like the other surrounding nations. God informed Samuel to grant their demand. Although Saul was the king, he was not a carrier of the promise. God had chosen David, son of Jessie, to continue the bloodline of Adam through Abraham. The interesting thing about this covenant was that its continuation did not depend on obedience, only the faithfulness of God. The focus of it was the establishment of God's kingdom boundaries. This covenant continued until a better one (the new covenant) was enforced. Unlike the Abrahamic covenant, the Davidic covenant was stained with disobedience, rejections, and unbelief, which could only be understood by the law of sin and death.

The Fifth Covenant: The New Covenant

The fifth and final covenant is one that stands on grace, acceptance, and belief. The new covenant is a transformation of the true intent of God's relationship with all his people for which he justified and glorified. Those individuals he predestinated from the beginning. This covenant was declared in the garden to the serpent as a punishment. The seed of the woman, which is the promise, is the sum total of all the covenants God had made with man. Paul tells us that the seed mentioned in Genesis 17:8 is Christ (Gal. 3:16). As mentioned earlier, Christ is the physical image of God, God in the flesh—the living soul, God's representative on earth who is the caretaker with the position and status of king and priest. The old covenant was presented by the blood of animals; however, the new covenant was presented by the blood of Christ. It is the blood of Christ Jesus that cleanses us from sin (1 John 1:7). Therefore, the new covenant is sealed with the blood of Christ and cannot be undone, making it an everlasting covenant.

Is My Gospel WOKE?
(World Over Kingdom Evermore)

The primary belief about WOKE-ness is that something is wrong. For thousands of years, human society has had one problem or another. For that same amount of time, we have been seeking answers. Up to now, no one can come up with a reason why. Why then is this, could it be that there is no human answer to be gotten?

Could it be that it is right around the corner waiting to manifest itself? Is it possible that we are looking in the wrong places? It is funny how the leaders who have been in the middle of this now appear not to know what to do. They are now looking dumbfounded while engaging in an age-old question. Have they not been the ones who said over and over again that you just follow me and all will be okay? This brings me back to one of the aforementioned questions: Are we looking in the wrong places for answers? Well, this question leads down two separate paths: one down the secular road and the other down the religious road. However, just as mentioned before, they are like a train track; they both run parallel but do not cross. Now we must understand that within both the secular and religious environments, there are subsections of tracks that are good and evil.

Let us explore this further.

What is down these paths? The only reference I can come up with is the Holy Bible. The Bible, which is a book of war and warnings, continuously tells us of the conflicts between good and evil. It talks about how evil is forever trying to overcome good. Paul tells us in Galatians 5, "For the flesh lusteth against the Spirit, and the Spirit against the flesh: and these are contrary the one to the other: so that ye cannot do the things that ye would." If God tells us there is a conflict, then a conflict it shall be. Presently, society is becoming "WOKE." To be WOKE is to become aware of injustices with a strong feeling to correct them. A classic meaning of "WOKE" is "WORLD OVER KINGDOM EVERMORE." Person who has become WOKE always looks for something they feel is unjust. More on this later. We must understand that the secular world is occupied by the children of darkness. Their job is to kill, steal, and destroy just like their father. This is so because they are of their father, the devil. The secular world has not just entered into darkness, but they have been there since the beginning. They got that way when their father, Cain (who was of the wicked one), killed his brother and lied about it to God. Reminder, in 1 John 2:16, we are told, "For all that is in the world, the lust of the flesh, and the lust of the eyes, and the pride of life, is not of the Father, but is of the world." Therefore, to follow the secular world is to follow the children of disobedience. This is because their objective is to get things and stuff through fear. They operate under the philosophy and vain deceit, after the tradition of men, after the rudiments of the world, and not after Christ. They are "WOKE." We are told in Ephesians 5:6–10, "Let no man deceive you with vain words: for because of these things cometh the wrath of God upon the children of disobedience. Be not ye, therefore, partakers with them. For ye were sometimes darkness, but now are ye light in the Lord: walk as children of light: [For the fruit of the Spirit is in all goodness and righteousness and truth] Proving what is acceptable unto the Lord."

The world is a dangerous place, full of chaos and voidness. Now as mentioned before, 1 Corinthians 5:9–13 states, "I wrote unto you in an epistle not to company with fornicators: Yet not altogether with the fornicators of this world, or with the covetous, or extortioners, or with idolaters; for then must ye needs go out of the world. But now I have written unto you not to keep company, if any man that is called a brother be a fornicator, or covetous, or an idolator, or a railer, or a drunkard, or an extortioner; with such an one no not to eat. For what have I to do to judge them also that are without? do not ye judge them that are within? But them that are without God judgeth. Therefore put away from among yourselves that wicked person."

Now then, who are their leaders? Second Timothy 3 identifies them and their mission as, "This know also, that in the last days perilous times shall come. For men shall be lovers of their selves, covetous, boasters, proud, blasphemers, disobedient to parents, unthankful, unholy, Without natural affection, trucebreakers, false accusers, incontinent, fierce, despisers of those that are good, Traitors, heady, high-minded, lovers of pleasures more than lovers of God; Having a form of godliness, but denying the power thereof: from such turn away. For of this sort are they which creep into houses, and lead captive silly women laden with sins, led away with divers lusts, Ever learning, and never able to come to the knowledge of the truth. Now as Jannes and Jambres withstood Moses, so do these also resist the truth: men of corrupt minds, reprobate concerning the faith." The leaders of this sort is very "WOKE" and dangerous.

Peter informs us about Paul in 2 Peter 3:15–18, "And account that the longsuffering of our Lord is salvation; even as our beloved brother Paul also according to the wisdom given unto him hath written unto you; As also in all his epistles, speaking in them of these things; in which are some things hard to be understood, which they that are unlearned and unstable wrest, as they do also the other scriptures, unto their own destruction. Ye therefore, beloved, seeing ye know these things before, beware lest ye also, being led away with the error of the wicked, fall from your own stedfastness. But grow in grace, and in the knowledge of our Lord and Saviour Jesus Christ. To him be glory both now and forever. Amen." Matthew confirms the vulnerability of even the elect when he writes in chapter 24:22–24, "And except those days should be shortened, there should no flesh be saved: but for the elect's sake those days shall be shortened. Then if any man shall say unto you, Lo, here is Christ, or there; believe it not. For there shall arise false Christs, and false prophets, and shall shew great signs and wonders; insomuch that, if it were possible, they shall deceive the very elect." Therefore, be careful that you know who and whose you are and do not follow the voice of a stranger.

After reviewing the above narrative, a question enters my mind. That question is, Does God want humanity to be confused? If so, why? As I was searching the scriptures, I found something interesting in the book of Genesis. Genesis 11 answered several questions for me, including the one just mentioned. The answered to the above question may be found in the first nine verses of that chapter. For remembrance's sake, let's review. This is the time after the flood, and Noah and his family began to expand the Adamic covenant of being fruitful, multiplying, replenishing, subduing, and having dominion over the earth. Genesis 10:32 states that "these are the families of the sons of Noah, after their generations, in their nations: and by these were the nations divided in the earth after the flood." Now to continue with Genesis 11:1–9. We are told, "And the whole earth was of one language, and of one speech. And it came to pass, as they journeyed from the east, that they found a plain in the land of Shinar; and they dwelt there. And they said one to another, Go to, let us make brick, and burn them thoroughly. And they had brick for stone, and slime had they for morter. And they said, Go to, let us build us a city and a tower, whose top may reach unto heaven; and let us make us a name, lest we be scattered abroad upon the face of the whole earth. And the Lord came down to see the city and the tower, which the children of men builded. And the Lord said, Behold, the people is one, and they have all one language; and this they begin to do: and now nothing will be restrained from them, which they have imagined doing. Go to, let us go down, and there confound their language, that they may not understand one another's speech. So the Lord scattered them abroad from thence upon the face of all the earth: and they left off to build the city. Therefore is the name of it called Babel; because the Lord did there confound the language of all the earth: and from thence did the Lord scatter them abroad upon the face of all the earth."

Two things in these scriptures I found interesting: one is that the people had a fear of being scattered abroad on the earth in verse 4. And the other is in verse 7 when God confounds their language so they could not build the city and tower and get to heaven. Looking at verse 4, the people wanted to get to heaven. They felt or understood that they needed to be close to God. Did they want to get close to God to be gods, be more like God, or to show God what they had learned and was able to do? Anyway, they felt the need to get close to God and make them a name. Question, What is the importance of making a name? Having the right name is very important to God. We find in Revelation 2:17 that God says, "He that hath an ear, let him hear what the Spirit saith unto the churches; To him that over-cometh will I give to eat of the hidden manna, and will give him a white stone, and in the stone a new name written, which no man knoweth saving he that receiveth it. Now to those who hear what the Spirit saith will get a stone with a new name in it." Could this be what the people in Genesis 11 was talking about? You do remember that this is after the flood that cleansed the earth of all those who were wicked.

Now I find it intriguing that God in verses 7 and 8 confound the languages and cause them to do the very thing they were afraid of: being scattered abroad the face of all the earth and forgetting about building a tower. Now in connection to the question of "Does God want the people to be confused?" our teachings today is that our objective is to get where God is in heaven. We are taught that, one day, the Lord will come and take us home. Also, our teachings tells us that we are to become unified as one, just like it is in heaven. However, is that what God wants? Because if it is, why did he do what he did? In Genesis 2, we find that God at the forming of the man gave him a purpose—that purpose was to till (take care of the) ground outside the garden. That purpose (which has not changed) could not be fulfilled if they were grouped in one place or escape to somewhere else. What is your perspective?

Another fascinating thing that happened in this chapter is that the only family line from here out is the line of Shem, which leads to Abraham. Could this be what the book of Jasher talks about when it is called the *Book of the Just Ones* or the *Upright Ones* (*Strong's Concordance* H3477)? This is important because Abraham's line leads to Judah. In Genesis 49:9–10, when Jacob calls his sons before him to tell them what they could suspect in the last days, he told Judah this, "Judah, thou art he whom thy brethren shall praise: thy hand shall be in the neck of thine enemies; thy father's children shall bow down before thee. Judah is a lion's whelp: from the prey, my son, thou art gone up: he stooped down, he couched as a lion, and as an old lion; who shall rouse him up? The sceptre shall not depart from Judah, nor a lawgiver from between his feet, until Shiloh come; and unto him shall the gathering of the people be." Jacob pronounced on him that his line would produce the holder of the everlasting scepter, Shiloh. Shiloh, who *Strong's Concordance* (H7886) identifies as "he whose it is, that which belongs to him, tranquility." This is Jesus, the Christ, the Living Soul, the Son of God, the Lion of the Tribe of Judah. All this is interesting at a very high level. However, can we find another time when God scattered the people when the people did not want to be scattered? Throughout the Bible, we find instances where God had to push the people to action, many times, because they were influenced by leaders who did or did not under-stand the purpose of man, who were knowingly or unknowingly were dishonoring God. Now a classic example of this is in Acts 11:18–21, where we are informed that "when they heard these things, they held their peace, and glorified God, saying, Then hath God also to the Gentiles granted repentance unto life. Now they which were scattered abroad upon the persecution that arose about Stephen travelled as far as Phenice, and Cyprus, and Antioch, preaching the word to none but unto the Jews only. And some of them were men of Cyprus and Cyrene, which, when they were come to Antioch, spake unto the Grecians, preaching the Lord Jesus. And the hand of the Lord was with them: and a great number believed, and turned unto the Lord." I think the best example of this is in Genesis 41, when the famine forced the children of Israel to go to Egypt for food. God did this for we find in Genesis 46 when God spoke to Israel and said this, "So Israel set out on the journey with everything he owned. He arrived at Beersheba and worshiped, offering sacrifices to the God of his father Isaac. God spoke to Israel in a vision that night: 'Jacob! Jacob!,' 'Yes?' he said. 'I'm listening.' God said, 'I am the God of your father. Don't be afraid of going down to Egypt. I'm going to make you a great nation there. I'll go with you down to Egypt; I'll also bring you back here. And when you die, Joseph will be with you; with his own hand he'll close your eyes'" (MSG). There many other instances where God moved believers when they did not want or did not know what to do. Let us not lose focus on the primary question of "What is wrong?". From my perspective, to say something is wrong concerning humanity is to say God does not know what he is doing (this is only my perspective).

This journey in Genesis 11 has opened up the view into other areas of human societies. The first nine verses of the chapter indicate that the imagination of man is a powerful attribute. It further indicates the need for a proper mindset—a mindset that is of God. But there can be no mindset of God if there is no Spirit of God. Remember, in Genesis 6, God said his Spirit would not always be with men (H120) for they are wicked. The wickedness of man is that they have no godly spiritual guidance. It is possible that they are "WOKE." However, he found Noah who was righteous because of his righteous bloodline and mindset that came from Adam, the living soul, which was in right standing with God. Now it was that bloodline that preserved to seed that carried the Spirit of God. Therefore, Noah became the first seed bearer of the woman to carry forth the Adamic covenant and God's plan of destroying the works of the devil. And that seed was passed down to Shem and the chosen of his descendants until Jesus. However, many of the descendants of Noah were left to their own devices (no spirit of God). A closer understanding of this will lead us to the development of the races. We find in Genesis 10 that there was a scattering of the sons of Noah to various parts of the earth. For example, sons of Japheth settle in the islands of the Gentiles in the north (Genesis 10:5). The sons of Ham settle in the Middle East around the land of Canaan while the sons of Shem settle in the area of Arabia. The interesting thing here is the secular world identifies this action via the dictionary as those people from the far east were once known as "Mongoloids" (no longer in technical use), which means "relating to, or characteristic of one of the traditional racial divisions of humankind." Those who were from the region of Africa were known as "Negroid" (no longer in technical use), which relates to "the characteristics of the peoples traditionally classified as the Negro race." And those in the north were known as "Caucasians" (no longer in technical use), which relates to "the characteristics of one of the traditional racial divisions of humankind." As we can see, the secular world divides humanity by skin color and physical characteristics while God did no such thing. The reason God separated them was to do the purpose he assigned them to do. Also, God separated them by language, not skin color. This now brings up the term "racism." The primary question is, Is it of the world or God? Here is a classic case of the world taking something of God and perverting it.

As we look around in society today, we find there are many conflicting things happening. The legalization of late-term abortion, the rise of intersectionality, critical race theory, the secret war of men versus women, the constant attempt to invade our Christian beliefs, and the overall effort to overrun the country by illegal immigrants are but a few things that are designed to sew division and discord. As we look at these attributes of today's society, we find those who partake in these actions are considered "WOKE" and enlighten to the ways of the world.

Could these things be proving the Scriptures to be right about the last days? First John tells us that the antichrist is coming, and they are already here. We are warned that the ministers of Satan will come as ministers of righteousness, whose destruction is near. Here, John says the are many antichrists, and they are here now. What then is an antichrist? *Strong's Concordance* G500 tells us that they are "the adversary of the Messiah; simply put, haters of Jesus." Jesus has warned us to be ready for all types of deceptions. Primarily, the one being the ravening wolves in sheep clothing. However, to me, the greatest indication of all that the last days are here is that supposedly children of God are standing up for the separation of people by race or sex. Wait a minute, are these the ravening wolves? Many of them are doing this to fit in with modern society. They have been already or becoming "WOKE." Presently, they are disregarding Ephesians 5:6–12, which reminds us, "Let no man deceive you with vain words: for because of these things cometh the wrath of God upon the children of disobedience. Be not ye therefore partakers with them. For ye were sometimes darkness, but now are ye light in the Lord: walk as children of light: [For the fruit of the Spirit is in all goodness and righteousness and truth] Proving what is acceptable unto the Lord. And have no fellowship with the unfruitful works of darkness, but rather reprove them. For it is a shame even to speak of those things which are done of them in secret." If a supposedly child of God participates with the children of darkness in unbelievers works to become "WOKE," then those people who do such may not be who they say they are. Just saying.

The works the children of darkness are using today is racism and sexism as their weapons of choice. Racism, which is defined as "one group exhibiting superiority over another group based on skin color and/or cultural beliefs" while sexism is defined as "attitudes or behavior based on traditional stereotypes of gender roles; discrimination or devaluation based on a person's sex or gender, as in restricted job opportunities, especially such discrimination directed against women; ingrained and institutionalized prejudice against or hatred of women; misogyny." Racism and sexism have been proven to be very subjective. This is because they operate primarily on emotions, feelings, and opinions. Things that cannot be proven with facts. The only purpose that racism and sexism exists is to be used as a weapon to sew social division and chaos. As we look at intersectionality and critical race theory, which are theories based on assumptions and used to promote protests and riots, we find this example from a Facebook post by a state Democratic legislator:

> Someone asked me after the vote on the flag, What's next? It's not what's next, it is what continues. The flag change didn't happen in just these past few days. It took years for all to line up and work in favor of a flag change. So to answer the question what is next, well…today I will continue the work that will make available to all Mississippians affordable health care. I will continue working for equal pay for women in the workplace. I will continue to push for quality education for children in our state. I will continue to work towards laws that provide equitable opportunities for black businesses in our state. I will continue to work to get true prison reform. I will continue to push for teacher and state employee pay raises. I will continue to walk through the valleys and push aside obstacles that do not allow equity for those I serve and all of Mississippi. So when asked what is next, it is not what's next, it is what continues.

There was a comment to this post follow that went like this:

> Okay, this is an answer from one of the leaders that have been fighting this fight for years. My understanding of this is that they have beaten the flag issue, now let's move to the next one. Remember, this is only one of the local leaders of this cultural

revolution and only their agenda. Now, let us take a closer look at their continuous fight.

First on the list is "health care for all." The question here is to define "all." Is it all American citizens? Anyone within American's borders (legal and illegal)? Or everyone in the world? Finally, who will pay for it?

Next on the list is equal pay of women in the workplace. Is not this statement in and of itself sexist? I think it has been proven that consideration for a pay scale is based on the negotiating parties. It was said that many women fail to negotiate properly when engaged in this process. Also, whatever happened to the privacy of pay? Is it right to be comparing an individual's pay scale with others? Under the American workplace system (the old one) of pay is based on what an individual brings to the table and not what sex they are? Anyway.

As we go on, they want quality education of the children within our state. My question here is, Who is at fault that our children are not getting a quality education? Is it the parents, the teachers, the government, or the students? Also, when did this become a problem, and why was is not fixed when it started? Who is the blame? Again, the parents, the teachers, the government, or the students? Where does education begin? Who determines what is important for our children to know? You know the answers to these questions. Just look in the past—that's right! We are erasing the past for a new social culture.

Okay, now we are going to ensure equitable opportunities for Black businesses. Does this mean Black businesses get special privileges over others? If this is the case then, isn't that Black privilege that stems from Black supremacy, or are you implying that Black businesses are inferior to others and need special help? Confusing to me. Is the objective here for Black businesses to be equal or superior over others?

Next on the list is prison reform. Where does prison reform begin? In the home, in the street, or prison? The same questions need to be asked that was asked about quality education. Whose fault is it, and when did it start, and why it was not fixed then? What then is the solution? Retry all prisoners for new sentences? Reform the court and ensure judges consider race when sentencing? Or close down the prisons altogether and let them go to reform school?

As we continue, pay raises for teachers and state workers. Teaching is an important profession within our society. In the past, I think teachers got into that profession to help our children grow up to be respectable citizens and produced positively in the community. The ones I grew up with did it from the heart (spirit) and not from the pocket (money). Many of them were Christians and knew God would supply their needs and not the government (oh, that's a thing of the path that is being erased). As for state workers, if they feel they are not getting paid at the level they think, let them go to the private sector and compete. Let them bring their skills to the table (that's the way it was in the past).

Finally, down in the valley with my people. Those people who feel they have obstacles in their way that they cannot succeed in life. Those who know they are not economically, politically,

educationally, and whatever else you can put in
the pot of victimization equal with others.

What I find interesting in all this is that there is no mention of who the enemy is that they are fighting to overcome and take their place. This is intriguing because, in the fight for the flag, the enemy was White supremacy that represented hatred. The solution then was to fight hatred with hatred. The only thing hatred bring is division and separation. There was a hatred for the flag that was so powerful that it made people sick in the mind to the point they became that which they were fighting. Now is that the truth, or is this whole cultural revolution is based on a lie and the leaders have a far-reaching agender? Read the legislator's words. This is just the beginning. Defeat the enemy whomever it or they may be. If they do not have one, they will make one up.

Although there is no Jesus mentioned in this campaign for righteousness, to those of you who consider themselves believers, remember what Paul said in Colossians 2:8, "Beware lest any man spoil you through philosophy and vain deceit, after the tradition of men, after the rudiments of the world, and not after Christ." Everything in this legislator's words is of the world and belong to it. The same thing the woman saw in the tree and what 1 John 2:16 tells to believers, "For all that is in the world, the lust of the flesh, and the lust of the eyes, and the pride of life, is not of the Father, but is of the world."

As previously mentioned, leaders that are WOKE are now bringing a Christian twist of doing it because they care while adding the protest tactic of the civil rights movement of the sixties into the process.

Today, many of us are more than ready to label any incident between a White person and the person of color or woman as either a racial or sexist incident. Knowing that in doing so, they will incite the biases and prejudges of their base into an aggressive state. What I find troubling about this is that we now find (so-called) Christian leaders advocating racism and sexism. Many of them have chosen to become social justice activists, sewing discord rather than being leaders (ambassadors) of Christ that promote peace, tolerance, and reconciliation unto God. I must again warn those of you who are promoting these social justice agendas of racism and sexism that it is a dangerous thing. It is dangerous because its primary purpose is the divide and cause chaos, which is the work of darkness. Jesus tells us that a house that is divided will not stand. Another thing that is important concerning racism and sexism is that the core elements of them are superiority and inferiority. Therefore, anytime we use these terms, they activate those two elements into action—primarily for the bad.

Currently, we find the accusation of racism or sexism primarily comes from those who feel that they are being oppressed by someone or something. This also includes those that support their position of being oppressed or being the oppressor. Know the Spirit by the Spirit. They have a feeling that is based on the emotions and opinions of others. Many, if not all, of their accusations are void of facts and full of assumptions. When we assume something, we project our feeling, emotions, and opinions on it and began to see things as we want them to be and not as they are. And an oppressed person needs and oppressor to justify their actions of aggression. What then is the answer? The common answer to this question is that there is a lack of knowledge. Well then, who are those who have a lack of knowledge? Is it the Whites, the Blacks, the Asians, the Hispanics, or who? The funny thing about knowledge is that it has no color lines, it has no cultural lines, and it has no restrictions at all.

You see, knowledge is passed down. It is imparted and bestowed upon them that are chosen by God. Knowledge brings with it wisdom and understanding. Proverbs 2:6 tells us, "For the Lord giveth wisdom: out of his mouth cometh knowledge and understanding." In another Proverbs, we are told, "When wisdom enters into thine heart, and knowledge is pleasant unto thy soul; Discretion shall preserve thee, understanding shall keep thee." Can these things, we call racism and sexism, be a product of lack of knowledge? We are taught from Hosea 4:6, which says, "My people are destroyed for lack of knowledge." It must be noted here that Hosea is talking about Israel from an unbelieving position. Paul told us in Romans that Israel had a form of righteousness but not the righteousness of God. This indicates that some have the knowledge and others do not. This Scripture tells us that the lack of knowledge destroys. The lack of knowledge of God is what destroys people. An important thing here is that it is God who imparts knowledge and understanding in us as he sees fit. If we take a closer look, the Scripture unfolds the real reason for the lack of knowledge. Hosea 4:6 continues, "My people are destroyed for lack of knowledge: because thou hast rejected knowledge, I will also reject thee, that thou shalt be no priest to me: seeing thou hast forgotten the law of thy God, I will also forget thy children." A biblical example of this can be found in Malachi 1:12–14, where the Lord said this, "But ye have profaned it, in that ye say, The table of the Lord is polluted; and the fruit thereof, even his meat, is contemptible. Ye said also, Behold, what a weariness is it! and ye have snuffed at it, saith the Lord of hosts; and ye brought that which was torn, and the lame, and the sick; thus ye brought an offering: should I accept this of your hand? saith the Lord. But cursed be the deceiver, which hath in his flock a male, and voweth, and sacrificeth unto the Lord a corrupt thing: for I am a great King, saith the Lord of hosts, and my name is dreadful among the heathen." It is clear here that the Lord was upset with someone. We are taught that God is a loving and forgiving God and that we have a free will to do what we want when we want. Maybe you need to look further into Malachi where we find God's reaction. In chapter 2:1–4, God pronounce his judgment, which is, "And now, O ye priests, this commandment is for you. If ye will not hear, and if ye will not lay it to heart, to give glory unto my name, saith the Lord of hosts, I will even send a curse upon you, and I will curse your blessings: yea, I have cursed them already, because ye do not lay it to heart. Behold, I will corrupt your seed, and spread dung upon your faces, even the dung of your solemn feasts; and one shall take you away with it. And ye shall know that I have sent this commandment unto you, that my covenant might be with Levi, saith the Lord of hosts." If a WOKE Christian leader think God is playing, you need to look at Acts 17, where Paul says, "In times past, God winked at ignorance, but he is commanding repentance."

We learn that it is not a lack of knowledge but a rejection of the knowledge of God. The people knew God, but their priest (leaders) had forgotten his ways. They had changed his glory into shame, which was a sin against him. Could we be experiencing the same thing today? A classic misinterpretation of Scriptures by today's leaders is in 2 Chronicles 7:14, which is a reply to Solomon by God, concerning God's relationship with his people. The verse says, "If my people, which are called by my name, shall humble themselves, and pray, and seek my face, and turn from their wicked ways; then will I hear from heaven, and will forgive their sin, and will heal their land." The conversation they were having concerned the people being redeemed if God did something to them. The phrase "turn from their wicked ways" stands out to me. Present-day teaching about this Scripture indicates that the children of Christ (God) has wicked ways and requires redemption. The question here is, What wickedness has the Children of God committed?

Many of our leaders, both secular and religious, have become social justice activists, changing the truth of God into a lie. I have found that many are teaching God's people from others interpretation of what God says. There is always someone who implies, "God said this, but he really meant that." Finally, we read in Romans 1:22–25, "Professing themselves to be wise, they became fools, and changed the glory of the incorruptible God into an image made like to corruptible man, and to birds, and four footed beasts, and creeping things. Wherefore God also gave them up to uncleanness through the lusts of their own hearts, to dishonor their own bodies between themselves: Who changed the truth of God into a lie, and worshipped and served the creature more than the Creator, who is blessed forever. Amen."

So, therefore, the reality of racism and sexism is that there is no reality of them to those who are called and chosen of the Lord Jesus, the Christ. Now if you are one of those who feel these "isms" are real and you declare yourself to be a child of God, God demands you take a good look at your position to determent if you are or not. Hebrews 5:12 states, "For when for the time ye ought to be teachers, ye have need that one teaches you again which be the first principles of the oracles of God; and are become such as have need of milk, and not of strong meat." The first principle of God is wisdom. Proverbs

4:7 states, "Wisdom is the principal thing; therefore get wisdom: and with all thy getting get understanding." God gives wisdom, and that wisdom is Jesus (1 Corinthians 1:24, "But unto them which are called, both Jews and Greeks, Christ the power of God, and the wisdom of God").

You may not know this, but anytime you place the noun "ism" behind another word, you turn that word into a doctrine, theory, system, or practice that governs a religion. Therefore, if you are a pastor or leader that promotes racism or sexism as being real, then you are a pastor or leader of a false doctrine, and your teachings are false. However, the question is still out there. *What is wrong?*

After engaging in conversations with several individuals about this question, I have found that many people do not have an absolute view of things. Anytime, absoluteness (free from imperfection; complete; perfect) comes up, they tend to want to sit on the fence and inject their personal feeling and emotions into the situation, attempting to destroy the percept. Many of them do not understand that to engage in a profitable conversation, the good of both sides must be sorted out to come to a compromising conclusion. An example of this is that many people say that the police need more training on how to deal with individuals in the community. But the other side of this is a failure to address the lack of respect for authority within many communities. In looking at things from one perspective or another, there is an atmosphere of the law versus lawlessness involve. Whenever law and lawlessness meet, the result is chaos. Therefore, the question presents itself as to who benefits from chaos. If you are a student of the Bible, then you know who is the author and finisher of chaos. Well, then one wrong thing is that many people walk in a world of emotions and feelings that produces confusion. Therefore, to enter into this atmosphere of chaos, you begin to walk in the darkness that is only designed to produce destruction. If you feel lawlessness is acceptable on any level, then you are the cause and not the solution. Paul tells us in 1 Corinthians that "all things are lawful unto me, but all things are not expedient: all things are lawful for me, but I will not be brought under the power of any." In other words, just because I have the right to do something does not mean I need to do it. He again tells us to study to show ourselves approved.

Another thing that may be wrong is the view of the purpose of the church. We have been taught that the church is a hospital for those in need of redemption. Sinners who need salvation from their sins. Several of our leaders preach to those who are not in the kingdom about how to come to the door of the kingdom (Jesus). Many of them fail to preach what it means to be in the kingdom of God. The view that the church is a hospital for the lost is a misrepresentation of the church as a sanctuary. What then is the difference between a hospital and a sanctuary? A hospital is a place for all to get temporary comfort from an illness or injury. The dictionary defines "hospital" as "an institution in which sick or injured persons are given medical or surgical treatment." I found it interesting that a sanctuary in the *Strong's Concordance* H6944 means "apartness, holiness, sacredness, separateness" for God. The root word H6942 means "to consecrate, sanctify, prepare, dedicate, be hallowed, be holy, be sanctified, be separate." My understanding of this is that those who go to a hospital, go to get well enough to go back to the conditions they came from while those who come to the sanctuary are sent there for protection. You do know that the church is like an embassy (a body of persons entrusted with a mission to a sovereign or government, especially an ambassador and his or her staff), and the ground it is on is the same as being in the kingdom of God. We are ambassadors of God and not doctors and nurses for sinners. The dictionary defines it as "a sacred or holy place." Now the question is, Can sinners and unholy spirits be welcome or enter in a sanctuary of God used by children of God? Second Corinthians 6:14 states, "Be ye not unequally yoked together with unbelievers: for what fellowship hath righteousness with unrighteousness? and what communion hath light with darkness?" I think (only my perspective) that the answer to the question of "what is wrong?" maybe many do not believe what they believe; let God be true. Maybe many are trying to become who they already are, or maybe they are trying to get where they are already at. Just saying. If this is true, then they are living in an atmosphere of confusion, never coming to the true knowledge and understanding of who and whose they are. But still, that question is out there for you. What is wrong? The things that are considered wrong in the world can be traced back to the garden. Remember, God's prophecy on the serpent that declared there would be a war between his seed and the seed of the woman. This means that evil will be continuously attempting to defeat the good. However, in the end, the good always wins.

What then is the objective of Christianity? We're taught that we are warriors for Christ. As warriors, we are to protect those who are less fortunate than we are. We are to be soul winners for the Lord leading the lost to Christ. Compelling them that their soul needs saving from their sins. And many times, informing them they are going to go to a devil's hell if they do not repent and see the light. However, many times, we get overzealous in our pursuit of sinners to the point of becoming addicted to the cause. This overzealousness makes Christians prime targets of those promoting intersectionality and critical race theory.

At this juncture, Paul explains in Romans 10:1–2, "Brethren, my heart's desire and prayer to God for Israel is, that they might be saved. For I bear them record that they have a zeal of God, but not according to knowledge." Many times, in our zealous state, we leave God out and interject our conjectures. This causes many to become legalistic in their religion. You do remember the story of Barabbas the Zealous? The question here is, Does the Bible tell us that all will be save? First John 2:19 says, "They went out from us, but they were not of us; for if they had been of us, they would no doubt have continued with us: but they went out, that they might be made manifest that they were not all of us." The answer to that question is, "No, it does not." There is a word in Matthew 7:20–23 that says, "Wherefore by their fruits ye shall know them. Not everyone that saith unto me, Lord, Lord, shall enter into the kingdom of heaven; but he that doeth the will of my Father which is in heaven. Many will say to me in that day, Lord, Lord, have we not prophesied in thy name? and in thy name have cast out devils? and in thy name done many wonderful works? And then will I profess unto them, I never knew you: depart from me, ye that work iniquity."

In 2 Thessalonians 2:7–11, we find this, "For the mystery of iniquity doth already work: only he who now letteth will let, until he be taken out of the way. And then shall that Wicked be revealed, whom the Lord shall consume with the spirit of his mouth, and shall destroy with the brightness of his coming: Even him, whose coming is after the working of Satan with all power and signs and lying wonders, And with all deceivableness of unrighteousness in them that perish; because they received not the love of the truth, that they might be saved. And for this cause God shall send them strong delusion, that they should believe a lie." Here, we find that there is something or someone that is holding back iniquity or, to be more exact, the wicked one. Who or what then is this protector? Some say it is the Holy Spirit, others say it is Jesus, and many just do not care. But the answer is in the objective of the social justice activists, which is to tear down the pillars of our societies. Many of which have already been infiltrated; however, the last one that is holding out is the church. There is an important note here. Within the institution of the church, there are two agencies: one being the tares, which can be classified as the organization of the church that follows man's rules and regulations, and the wheat, which is the organism of the church that follows God's New Testament Law.

The church is now under attack from within. I need to place a pin here. As I just stated, the church is under attack from within. The attack from within is that many who declare themselves as Christians are moving away from the basic doctrines of the early leaders. The basic teaching of Paul as outlined in 1st Corinthians 15, which follows, "Moreover, brethren, I declare unto you the gospel which I preached unto you, which also ye have received, and wherein ye stand; By which also ye are saved, if ye keep in memory what I preached unto you unless ye have believed in vain. For I delivered unto you first of all that which I also received, how that Christ died for our sins according to the scriptures; And that he was buried, and that he rose again the third day according to the scriptures." Paul goes on to tell us that the main point of Christianity is the resurrection; for without it, there is no Christianity. We find in many churches teaching about the resurrection that it is being replaced with how to get things and stuff. These are the things that Jude tells us to be aware of and gives us the responsibility to protect. However, let God be true; nothing caught God off guard. He tells us in 1st Timothy 4, "Now the Spirit speaketh expressly, that in the latter times some shall depart from the faith, giving heed to seducing spirits, and doctrines of devils; Speaking lies in hypocrisy; having their conscience seared with a hot iron; Forbidding to marry, and commanding to abstain from meats, which God hath created to be received with thanksgiving of them which believe and know the truth." Once again, I digress, sorry. Let's continue with the church is removed. At some point, God will remove her by the Holy Spirit, and all hell will temporarily break out. First Thessalonians 4:16–18 states that "for the Lord himself shall descend from heaven with a shout, with the voice of the archangel, and with the trump of God: and the dead in Christ shall rise first: Then we which are alive and remain shall be caught up together with them in the clouds, to meet the Lord in the air: and so shall we ever be with the Lord. Wherefore comfort one another with these words." I found in Acts 17:4–6 that Paul and Silas turned the world upside down with the interjection of Jesus's teachings. Is the world only returning to its original state of chaos? So in conclusion, the answer to the question of "what is wrong?", the answer is nothing. Because everything is right on schedule with the Lord's plan. So how then are we, as believers, to deal with and respond to the chaotic world? In 1 Corinthians 5:9–13, Paul appears to reverse his teachings on how we are to deal with the wicked world. In these verses, he says, "I wrote unto you in an epistle not to company with fornicators: Yet not altogether with the fornicators of this world, or with the covetous, or extortioners, or with idolaters; for then must ye needs go out of the world. But now I have written unto you not to keep company, if any man that is called a brother be a fornicator, or covetous, or an idolator, or a railer, or a drunkard, or an extortioner; with such an one no not to eat. For what have I to do to judge them also that are without? do not ye judge them that are within? But, them that are without God judgeth. Therefore put away from among yourselves that wicked person."

Paul tells us here that he was not talking about the wicked ones (children of darkness) because we need to deal with them from a business perspective. However, it is those in the church that are doing wicked things that we are to separate from. He goes on the say in these verses that we are to take care of those who are within and God will take care of those that are without. The winning of the souls that we are to get are those within our midst that are lost. Paul wrote why this is important in the verses before these in 1 Corinthians 5:1–8: "It is reported commonly that there is fornication among you, and such fornication as is not so much as named among the Gentiles, that one should have his father's wife. And ye are puffed up, and have not rather mourned, that he that hath done this deed might be taken away from among you. For I verily, as absent in body, but present in spirit, have judged already, as though I were present, concerning him that hath so done this deed, In the name of our Lord Jesus Christ, when ye are gathered together, and my spirit, with the power of our Lord Jesus Christ, To deliver such an one unto Satan for the destruction of the flesh, that the spirit may be in the day of the Lord Jesus. Your glorying is not good. Know ye not that a little leaven leaveneth the whole lump? Purge out therefore the old leaven, that ye may be a new lump, as ye are unleavened. For even Christ our passover is sacrificed for us: Therefore let us keep the feast, not with old leaven, neither with the leaven of malice and wickedness; but with the unleavened bread of sincerity and truth."

In this reading, the key phrase here is, "And ye are puffed up, and have not rather mourned, that he that hath done this deed might be taken away from among you." In the modern church, we find some things are being allowed that is an offense to God. One thing I can think of is the introduction of intersectionality and critical race theory, which are secular social teachings. Paul further informs us in 2 Corinthians 13:5–7 that we are to examine ourselves that we are in the faith and know that we are not reprobates. Christianity is a way of life that is wrapped in absoluteness. The absolute understanding that Jesus is the only true living God, God in the flesh (Romans 10:9), and the only way into the kingdom of God is through him (John 6:44).

Understand what John 10:39–40 says, "Therefore they could not believe, because that Esaias said again, He hath blinded their eyes, and hardened their heart; that they should not see with their eyes, nor understand with their heart, and be converted, and I should heal them." So if your gospel is based on a philosophy that conflicts with God's Word, then you are "WOKE." Where is your help? Study and listen to the Lord. Amen.

How Does Culture Plays into the Gospel?

As we move into this "WOKE" period in our country, we find that it always involves cultural conflicts. The conflict is identified as "culture wars." The act of one culture attempting to overtake another one by any means necessary. At this time, this culture war has entered into the church. To understand how this culture war is affecting our gospel society, we must take a look at the development of a culture.

This word "culture" comes with several definitions. One of the most declared by my research is, "Culture is the characteristics and knowledge of a particular group of people, encompassing language, religion, cuisine, social habits, music, and arts...." The word "culture" derives from a French term, which in turn derives from the Latin "colere," which means "to tend to the earth and grow, or cultivation and nurture." The first thing we must notice is a culture is comprised of characteristics and knowledge of something. In the dictionary, "culture" means "the quality in a person or society that arises from a concern for what is regarded as excellent in arts, letters, manners, scholarly pursuits, etc. A particular form or stage of civilization, like that of a certain nation or time: development or improvement of the mind by education or training." As shown in the definition of culture, it is made up of various categories. These categories define the characteristics of a group or a person. Knowing a culture is determined by the development of the mentioned categories, the question then is, How is it created and by whom? A culture is developed along two basic types, which are material culture, physical things produced by a society, and nonmaterial culture, intangible things produced by a society. Cars would be an example of American material culture while our devotion to equality is part of our nonmaterial culture. Therefore, a culture is developed by individuals within a group with the same goals in mind based on their characteristics and knowledge. The collective joining of ideas for the betterment of a group determines the success or failure of a culture. Now once those ideas are placed into motion by those individuals, culture then becomes a society.

The coming together of a culture to become a society is based on the structure of that society's rules and regulations that governed its membership acceptance. Therefore, a society is defined as "an organized group of persons associated together for religious, benevolent, cultural, scientific, political, patriotic, or other purposes"—a body of individuals living as members of a community. As we can see, a culture is the center of a society that makes that society a community. Therefore, within any society (community), there must be a hierarchy or governing body. The duties of that governing body is to establish guidelines that ensure the survival of the society. The important thing about the development of a community is that there must be established borders. Therefore, the job of the governing body is to ensure the survival of the society without infringing on the borders of another community. The objective of not infringing on another society's borders is a hard thing to do. The primary reason it is a hard thing to do is that each society develops into a community that is either classified as hunter-gatherers or agricultural. In an article from *Sparknotes—Society and Culture* (https://www.sparknotes.com/sociology/society-and-culture/section2/), an agricultural society, also known as an agrarian society, is a society that constructs social order around a reliance upon farming. More than half the people living in that society make their living by farming. An agricultural society is interesting in that the key characteristics of it is economy, wealth, and the society, in general, is centered primarily on agriculture. Human and animal labor are the primary tools employed for an agricultural society to survive.

The classification known as hunter-gatherers is defined as "a human living in a society in which most or all food is obtained by foraging [collecting wild plants and pursuing wild animals]." Hunter-gatherer societies stand in contrast to agricultural societies, which rely mainly on domesticated species. Hunting and gathering was humanity's first and most successful adaptation, occupying at least 90 percent of human history. Following the development of agriculture, hunter-gatherers who did not change have been displaced or conquered by farming or pastoralist groups in most parts of the world. Only a few contemporary societies are classified as hunter-gatherers, and many supplement their foraging activity with horticulture or pastoralism. Hunter-gatherers has some basic characteristics which are the following:

The primary institution is the family, which decides how food is to be shared and how children are to be socialized, and which provides for the protection of its members.

- They tend to be small with fewer than fifty members.
- They tend to be nomadic, moving to new areas when the current food supply in a given area has been exhausted.
- Members display a high level of interdependence.
- Labor division is based on sex: men hunt, and women gather.

It must be noted that, today, hunter-gatherer societies have just about faded away. They have been replaced by horticultural and pastoral societies. The death of the hunter-gatherer society was because of them becoming domesticated and integrated into agricultural societies. The interesting thing about this is that in Africa in the fifteenth, sixteenth, seventeenth, eighteenth, and some of the nineteenth centuries hunter-gatherer societies were many. However, the rise of more predominant Black agricultural societies and their need for labor, hunter-gatherers became an excellent source of labor; however, they needed to be domesticated.

There are many examples of this in human history. We can go back to the beginning with Cain, who was a farmer, killing Abel, who was a shepherd, because of anger. Throughout the biblical world, there were conquests, such as the Battle in the Vale of Siddim when all the kings gathered together to conqueror the kings of Sodom,

Gomorrah, Zeboiim, and Zoar for to take their land and enslave their people. Saul and David had many battles with their neighboring kingdoms primarily for the expansion of land, the modern-day history of Germany and Japan expanding their areas of influence, the Iranians going into Greece for conquest. Alexander the Great conquest of the Middle East, the British making colonies all over the world—all these activities were based on the needs of a specific culture to expand and survive. Conquest has always been the goal of man's survival plan.

Now back to the main question of this narrative, How does culture plays into the gospel? To go further into this question, I must ask, What is my culture? Well, I must first identify my ethnicity. I am an American of Black skin color. My existence as an American began in 1951. However, I can only trace my culture back to a time known as the Black slavery period. This was a period in time when there was a need for a cheap labor force—a time during the agricultural period in the South and the industrial period in the North in America. During that time, the cheapest and easiest form of labor was the domestication of people. Therefore, slavery was the means to accomplish that task. Now it must be understood that this practice (although completely legal but was completely unjust) was common within human history. The dictionary meaning of "slave" is "a person who is the legal property of another and is forced to obey them," also, "a person who works very hard without proper remuneration or appreciation," and "who is excessively dependent upon or controlled by something." Within the context of slavery, no designated race determined who was and who wasn't. Interesting, is it not? I have come to understand that the arrival of Black Africans, and many others, in America was solely for economic purposes. Yes! Black Africans were not the only people in slavery in America at the time. Therefore, the characteristics of the slave society were based on hard labor with the knowledge that they always needed an oppressor because their society dictated that they were oppressed. This mindset was embedded into some of them when they were domesticated by the Black Africans agricultural societies before being sold to other societies around the world. The only relief from the hard labor was when the oppressor saw fit. The only thing that the Black slave culture produced was a continuous need to fight the oppressor by any means necessary—a fight that continues on today against a real or an imaginary oppressor. Because this is the primary way, we know how to expand our influence over other societies. We have found via the civil rights experience that the primary way to overtake or influence another society is to provoke the fear of chaos into them. The success of this tactic moved my culture into a society of those in a perpetual state of need at its core. This cultural characteristic has developed into a category of science known as victimhood—a science that is a product of "intersectionality." This theory comes out of "critical race theory." Intersectionality is the tactic being used to resurrect a hunter-gather tribal mindset. Therefore, it has turned our culture into a culture based on using fear of the mob as a tactic of conquest. There are two primary weapons used within this tactic: they are racism and sexism. Before we continue, let us clarify some things. The definition of a "theory" is "a proposed explanation whose status is still conjectural and subject to experimentation in contrast to well-established propositions that are regarded as reporting matters of fact." Here, we find that a theory is based on conjectures and is under constant experimentation. We further find that a theory is not based on facts. Being that it is primarily based on conjectures, then what is a conjecture? An interesting thing about a conjecture is that it is "the formation or expression of an opinion or theory without sufficient evidence for proof—an opinion or theory so formed or expressed, guess, speculation." So then, if intersectionality and critical race theory are only theories, therefore, they are void of facts and are always in a continuous experimentation mode. I have found that if something is in a perpetual state of experimentation, then there is never an end in sight. Being that these two theories need the elements of an oppressor and an oppressed, then it would be impossible to come to an adequate and fair conclusion unless one of the elements is eliminated. Is the objective of intersectionality and critical race theory is to cause continuous chaos and confusion? If so, why? Just asking.

Let us take a look at "intersectionality." Intersectionality is "the theory that the overlap of various social identities, as race, gender, sexuality, and class, contributes to the specific type of systemic oppression and discrimination experienced by an individual [often used attributively]." Being that intersectionality is a theory, it within itself is not based on facts but is only a supposition (an assumption). The assumption (supposition) is that there is always someone or something being oppressed by someone or something. If this is the case, then there is never a resolution to any situation concerning the overlapping of cultures. Interesting. Where did this theory come from?

As we look around the world, starting from the beginning after the flood, the overlapping of cultures has been a normal part of man's existence. The problem then arises from the natures of good and evil. Evil has always attempted to overcome good. The Holy Scriptures tell us that conflict between good and evil will be a way of life until the Messiah comes. This is the prophecy that God cursed the serpent; with that, there would be enmity between him and the woman—a fight to the end. So we find that intersectionality is the latest evolution in the "evil versus good" fight. This old/new induction into the fight is from the mind of a legal scholar named Kimberlé Crenshaw in 1989. Ms. Crenshaw defined intersectionality as "a prism to bring to light dynamics within discrimination law that weren't being appreciated by the courts." Crenshaw said, "In particular, courts seem to think that race discrimination was what happened to all black people across genders, and sex discrimination was what happened to all women, and if that is your framework, of course, what happens to black women and other women of color is going to be difficult to see." Intersectionality is based on discrimination within the judicial system. It started as an assumption that the judicial system was unfair to women of color. The case was filed by Mrs. Emma Degraffenreid against General Motors, St. Louis, Missouri, in 1976. In this memorandum, we find that the basis of the sue was that Black women were discriminated against because of the hiring and firing policy was not to their advantage. The court found that the women could not cite an instance where racial or sexual discrimination existed. Based on the finding, the court would not declare Black women "a new super-remedy" because nothing was indicating the Black women had a special class status that protected them from discrimination.

In 1989, Ms. Crenshaw started her "intersectionality campaign." In a paper she titled "Demarginalizing the Intersection of Race and Sex: A Black Feminist Critique of Antidiscrimination Doctrine, Feminist Theory, and Antiracist Politics" (Kimberle Crenshaw, University of Chicago Legal Forum, volume 1989, issue 1, article 8; Kimberle.Crenshaw@chicagounbound.edu).

Ms. Crenshaw wrote the paper because she was dissatisfied with the conclusion of the court. In her mind, race and sex should have been combined to indicate the intersectionality or overlapping of the charge, thereby moving it into a new area of discrimination. This supposition or theory did not go anywhere until as Ms. Crenshaw in an article titled "The Highlight by Vox," on May 28, 2019, where the writer wrote, "But then something unexpected happened. Crenshaw's theory went mainstream, arriving in the Oxford English Dictionary in 2015 and gaining widespread attention during the 2017 Women's March, an event whose organizers noted how women's 'intersecting identities' meant that they were 'impacted by a multitude of social justice and human rights issues.' As Crenshaw told me, laughing, 'the thing that's kind of ironic about intersectionality is that it had to leave town'—the world of the law—'in order to get famous.'" Now based on the fact that intersectionality was rooted in the theory (assumption) of a person, then hijacked by social justice activists, who then tied it to the civil rights experience, causing the Black culture to form it into a social justice society?

Intersectionality has now been integrated into many areas of American society as a mainstream factual analytical tool. The question is, An analytical tool for what? Intersectionality is an open-ended assumption (theory) that is rooted in conflict. Therefore, for intersectionality to exist in a society, there must be perpetual oppressors to oppress those who are in a supposedly lower class. A never-ending story. In and of itself, intersectionality has become the new religion of defeating the enemy (oppressor) here and now by any means necessary. The primary concern I have with intersectionality is that it projects the culture of the past onto present day morals. In that, it holds the behaviors of those in the past to the standards of today. They indicate that the descendants of those in the past must atone for the actions of their ancestors. This request is an obscure one. The sins of the fathers are not the sins of the children.

Now although I do not subscribe to intersectionality as it relates to critical race theory, it has (knowingly or unknowingly) become the main focus of much of Black society (communities). The main theme of this tactic of intersectionality within the Black culture is that someone owes us something, and it is time to pay. This is very sad because there is no personal responsibility attached to this theory.

This information is from https://www.vox.com/the-highlight /2019/5/20/18542843/intersectionality-conservatism-law-race-gen-der-discrimination.

Is There a Target?

The question of "is there a target?" is intriguing. Intersectionality has its sights on every aspect of society. As we aforementioned, culture is made up of various characteristics and knowledge. The characteristic of a culture that interests me is religion. That focus on Christian society. Present-day Christianity is made up of several similar but distinct denominations that have several different movements within them. These movements consist of the following:

- Evangelicalism (no other religious movement reshaped America quite like evangelicalism)
- Restorationism
- Pentecostalism
- Christian fundamentalism
- Charismatic movement

Being that these movements are based on solid doctrine, intersectionality has built a new movement alongside the traditional ones. This new movement is called "Progressive Christianity," which operates primarily in the area of Christian music and entertainment. The progressive movement is centered on an eight-pointed doctrine. You can view all eight on their website, https://progressivechristianity. org/the-8-points/.

The points that I found interesting was numbers 2 and 5 which states,

> 2. Affirm that the teachings of Jesus provide but one of many ways to experience "God," the Sacredness, Oneness, and Unity of life and that we can draw from diverse sources of wisdom, including Earth, in our spiritual journey;
>
> 5. Find grace in the search for understanding and believe there is more value in questioning with an open mind and open heart, than in absolutes or dogma.

If I was not mistaken, I would say the Progressive Christianity has elements of Wiccan in it. Wiccan also gets its wisdom and powers from the earth, wind, fire, and air elements. We find that Progressive Christianity searches for grace by perpetually questioning and dismissing the absolute or dogma of traditional Christianity.

Now my main concern is that within the traditional movements, there is a push to incorporate intersectionality and critical race theory into them. I recently noticed an article concerned intersectionality and critical race theory on a Southern Baptist website found at http://www.sbc.net/resolutions/2308/resolution-9-on-critical-race-theory-and-intersectionality.

This is the web page of the SBC resolutions committee. On it, I found that the SBC had incorporated critical race theory into their platform as analytical tools on race relations. I find this troubling because intersectionality and critical race theory are not bounded in absoluteness but assumptions. Christianity, as I understand it to be, is ground in absoluteness and inerrancy. Christianity cannot be a social justice tool of analysis because Jesus was not a social justice warrior. Anyway, as stated before, the church is under attack both from within and without. Study to show yourself approved.

CONCLUSION

Why Does This Matter?

Although this narrative can continue, this is a good place to come to a conclusion. The main question asked here of "Why does this matter?" and "Is the Gospel you are taught, the True Gospel of Christ?" has its own answer within you, the answer that lies within all of those who declare themselves to be believers. The seed of the Christ that is in each of us gives us the right to determine why it matters. It matters because of the chaos of the world always and will be with us until the return. Jesus said that we are in the world but not of it. What does that mean? It means that those he has chosen (Eph. 1:4) called out of darkness into the marvelous light are a chosen generation that is a royal priesthood, a holy nation, and a peculiar people. A royal priesthood is those who hear the voice and follow. The holy nation is the church, the *ekklesia*, the gathering of the citizens of God's kingdom. Our purpose has not changed from the forming and mandate given to the living soul. The purpose of populating this chaotic earth into the kingdom of God (Col. 1:13) which is at hand (Matt. 3:2). The Lord is saying today what he said and did through Moses in Exodus 32:25–28, "And when Moses saw that the people were naked; (for Aaron had made them naked unto their shame among their enemies) Then Moses stood in the gate of the camp, and said, Who is on the Lord's side? let him come unto me. And all the sons of Levi gathered themselves together unto him. And he said unto them, Thus saith the Lord God of Israel, Put every man his sword by his side, and go in and out from gate to gate throughout the camp, and slay every man his brother, and every man his companion, and every man his neighbour. And the children of Levi did according to the word of Moses:

and there fell of the people that day about three thousand men." If you think God is winking at your ignorance in these last days, then just keep on thinking that (Acts 17:30). All of this matters because many have taken Old Testament theology and mixed is into New Testament Christology and came up with man's expectation philology. The basic use of the science of psychology as an influencing tool to control the mind of people is a very dangerous thing. Christ did not use psychology to influence people; he used the truth, which makes us free from the bondage of disobedience, rejections, and the unbelief. The understanding of Christology lets us know we have the grace, acceptance, and belief that we have already pleased God. We can do all things through Christ that strengthens us, and no weapon can form against us, etc. "Beware lest any man spoils you through philosophy and vain deceit, after the tradition of men, after the rudiments of the world, and not after Christ" (Col. 2:8).

CITATIONS FOR GRAPHICS

The Genealogy of Jesus—Page 45—https://lincolnparkubf.org/blog/2016/12/5/the-genealogy-of-jesus

Lifespan of the Biblical Patriarch—Page 45—https://www.conformingtojesus.com/charts-maps/en/chronology_adam-abraham.htm

Adam to Noah—Page 46—https://lewisburgdistrictumc.org/

Noah to Abraham—Page 47—https://www.pinterest.com/pin/106538347414011595/

Lineage from Abraham to Jesus—Page 48—https://www.biblestudy.org/maps/map-of-lineage-from-abraham-to-jesus.html

McGregor's Theory X and Theory Y—Page 71—https://frontlinemanagementexperts.wordpress.com/2015/08/31/douglas-mcgregor-on-theory-x-and-theory-y/

Maslow's Hierarchy of Need—Page 74—https://digital.com/how-to-become-an-entrepreneur/maslows-hierarchy/

The Adamic Covenant—Page 83—http://northside-bc.org/2015/11/29/the-adamic-covenant-genesis-1-3/

TheNoahicCovenant—Page85—https://www.goodsalt.com/details/pppas0083.html

The Abrahamic Covenant—Page 87—https://nhwchurch.ca/?s=abraham

The Davidic Covenant—Page 88—https://www.thecalvinist.net/post/1689-Baptist-Confession-Chapter-7:-Of-Gods-Covenant-Commentary#david

The New Covenant—Page 89—https://hoshanarabbah.org/blog/2019/11/28/new-covenant-or-renewed-covenant-what-are-its-terms-and-conditions/

ABOUT THE AUTHOR

Aaron Standberry was born in Jacksonville, FL, on the first day of June 1951. He is married to Dawn L. Standberry and has five (5) children—Cecelia Shabazz, Renaldo Pearson, John Standberry III (deceased), Keturah Standberry, and Hannah Standberry—and three (3) grandchildren. He serviced twenty-two years in the United States Air Force where he retired as a master sergeant (E7) security force weapons supervisor. After retirement, he took a position at Mississippi Gulf Coast Community College as a media services technician for twenty years. Aaron also worked at the local television station WLOX-TV 13 Biloxi, Mississippi, for fifteen years before completely retiring. He is a graduate of MGCCC with an associate degree in marketing management with a second associate degree in industrial security from the Air Force College. He also has a bachelor's degree in religion and business from William Carey University Harrisburg, MS. Aaron, along with his wife, is the founder/president of Jehovah Ministries, a 501c(3) ministry on the Mississippi Gulf Coast with the mission of providing a platform for local Christian ministries to spread the message via the multimedia broadcast industry. In his latter years, he is enjoying retirement and supports his church (First Baptist Church, Gulfport, MS) and the coastal community as a multimedia analyst.